GUNHAWK'S REVENGE

Jack Bannister, a legendary gun-slinger, wanders from town to town, hunting down the men who murdered his wife and daughter. His trail leads him to Hope Wells, where Jed Lacey, a member of the notorious Claver gang, faces a hangman's noose. When Marshal Ben Archer asks Bannister to be his deputy, he initially refuses and only pretty Kate Bonner can change his mind. Then the feisty Kate unmasks Jed Lacey as Luke Birch, the last man on Bannister's list. Now there would be hell to pay!

JACK HOLT

GUNHAWK'S REVENGE

Complete and Unabridged

LINFORD
Leicester

First published in Great Britain in 2001 by
Robert Hale Limited
London

First Linford Edition
published 2002
by arrangement with
Robert Hale Limited
London

British Library CIP Data

Holt, Jack
    Gunhawk's revenge.—Large print ed.—
Linford western library
    1. Western stories
    2. Large type books
    I. Title
    823.9'14 [F]

    ISBN 0–7089–9932–8

Published by
F. A. Thorpe (Publishing)
Anstey, Leicestershire

Set by Words & Graphics Ltd.
Anstey, Leicestershire
Printed and bound in Great Britain by
T. J. International Ltd., Padstow, Cornwall

This book is printed on acid-free paper

1

'Draw!'

Jack Bannister's fury-laden eyes bored into the quaking man standing twenty feet away in the wind-blown street. Frank Bains had been haunted for five years by a day that he knew was bound to come. After a visit to a doctor in San Antonio, almost a year before, he'd told himself that it didn't matter; the tumours in his lungs would get him before the man whose quest for revenge had earned him the appellation of Gunhawk would. However, now that he was about to die, he had a yearning for life — one more day — hell, even one more minute.

'You have a price to pay, Bains,' Gunhawk said. 'I'm here to collect.'

The sharp echo of Jack Bannister's exploding Peacemaker spread along the town's main street, bouncing off the clapboard buildings of the shabby enclave, diving into debris-strewn alleys, before rolling on into the black-faced hills beyond, scarred and pockmarked by dried-up claims left behind by prospectors who had not found the gold that the hills had promised a couple of years earlier. There were a lot of such towns in the mountains that had sprung up in hope, promised glory, and only delivered despair; places that became home to men like the man Bannister had come looking for, and had just killed.

Frank Bains clutched at his gut, his fingers desperately trying to gather together the ragged edges of the gaping hole that the Peacemaker's bullet had made. He looked to the cloud-enshrouded hills, his gaze far off, as his life ebbed away. He raised his eyes to meet Bannister's hard, pitiless stare, before the Peacemaker blasted him again. Bains fell on his face, ragged and bloodied.

'That leaves one more,' Bannister

murmured grimly.

Doors began to open cautiously, and folk drifted on to the ramshackle boardwalks in front of stores and houses that were part of the rot; Prosperity was a dead town and, come spring, when wagons could roll, a couple or more of its citizens would leave, and no one would come. So it would go on until Prosperity just folded up.

The door of the law office opened sluggishly, and an old-timer with fear-stalked eyes, toting a shotgun that Bannister reckoned would blow up in his face if triggered, stepped into the street.

'I told you to stay where you were old-timer,' Bannister called. 'Now I'm telling you to go back inside and finish that bottle I gave you when I visited. What's happened here is my business, and mine alone.'

'You just killed a man, mister,' the aged sheriff said. 'And that's darn well agin the law, even in this God forsaken hole.'

Jack Bannister said, 'My argument is not with you or this town, Sheriff. I've done what I've come to do. Now I'll be on my way.'

Nathan Jube's belly rumbled. He had just witnessed Bannister clear leather against Frank Bains, a fella who'd had a gun in his mitts since the cradle, and Bains hadn't stood a chance. He'd never seen a gun leave its holster as fast as Jack Bannister's had. He'd heard about the man called Gunhawk. He knew of his trail of revenge, spanning five years, in which each and every man who had tried to stop him had eaten dust. So, what was he doing standing in the middle of the street, in a no-consequence town, trying to implement a law that no one had cared about for quite a spell? A stand that would make him a candidate for a harp.

Pride and guilt. They were the reasons. Pride in the badge he wore, and for which he'd shown scant regard in recent times through a mixture of fear and despair. Guilt because he'd let a man be mercilessly gunned down. It made no difference that Frank Bains had needed killing for a long time.

He'd been a lawman all his life, spending time in some of the West's most lawless towns. He'd steadily drifted downwards as his skill and courage deserted him, until the year before he'd taken the sheriff's job in Prosperity. He figured that they'd named the place wrong; Dead End would have been a more appropriate name for a town that was more a graveyard.

He'd skulked, and let Bains be killed, telling himself that the lanky Texan would match Gunhawk, knowing deep down that he was lying to himself, because he hadn't the grit to try and stop Jack Bannister. No one would shed a tear for Frank Bains, he hadn't been one of God's better ideas. The fact was that even Frank Bains was entitled to the protection of the law, and he'd not given it. So, all that was left was to face his killer.

Bannister strode to his horse hitched to the rail outside the Goldpot, Prosperity's watering hole.

'Hold up, mister!' Jube ordered.

The man known as Gunhawk paused. His grey eyes as cold as winter frost considered the sheriff. He raised his hat and tucked in the ragged edges of his overlong raven-black hair.

'Let it be, old-timer,' he intoned. 'Frank Bains wasn't worth throwing away your life for.'

'This is a shotgun I'm pointing your way,' the sheriff said grittily. 'And a man ain't a pretty sight after a shotgun, mister.'

'You'll he in Heaven or Hell long before you'll get to pull the trigger,' Gunhawk said matter-of-factly, and walked on.

Nathan Jube's gut gave out a deeper rumble. 'I'm warning you, mister.' Bannister grabbed his saddle horn to vault into the saddle. 'That's it!' the sheriff called.

Quick as a snake-spit, Bannister spun around, Peacemaker clearing leather cocked and pointed, its trigger a shade off full pressure. Jube's eye hadn't been quick enough to match the speed of his draw. The sheriff sweated, as if he was plumb centre of the Mojave instead of snowy Montana. He waited for Jack Bannister's bullet to rip into him.

Bannister's sigh was world-weary. He holstered the Peacemaker and mounted his horse. Leaning into the stiffening wind, he rode on down Main, past Jube, and on into the coming blizzard gathering over the bleak, barren land-scape.

As the first snow-flurries whipped along the street, driven by a knife-sharp easterly, folk drifted back indoors. Jube, too, went back inside to finish off the bottle of whiskey that had put the iron in his legs to face Jack Bannister in the first place. But it wasn't courage he was now seeking from the liquor. It was forgetfulness.

Soon winter would virtually close Prosperity down. The snows would block the high pass that was the only way in and out, and everyone would wait out the dark days; eating little, because there was little to eat, and sleeping a lot because that's all there was to do.

Nathan Jube would promise himself a new start come spring. Everyone in the mountains did. It would never happen, of course. He'd made himself the same promise for the last six winters. He knew, though he wasn't yet ready to admit it, that he'd reached his last stop on a long trail.

He swayed to the window and looked out after the man called Gunhawk. He watched him into the distance, until the thickening snow made him one with the terrain; a spectre of death riding to collect his next soul. He fumbled his way to the cell that had been home to him since he'd arrived in Prosperity and flopped on to the bunk. He slugged the dregs of the whiskey, and let sleep overtake him; a sleep haunted by the man who had handed him back his miserable life, and hadn't done him any favour.

2

The *why* of Frank Bains's killing lay far back in Jack Bannister's past, but ever present, too. As close as the last raw second, in a heart that had festered for five years, poisoned by the bitterness that had begun in a small New Mexico town that hugged Arizona — a burg called Brody Creek.

Brody Creek was home to Jack Bannister, his wife Elizabeth and daughter Catherine. It had become so by chance when Elizabeth had been taken ill, and he had decided to leave the wagon train they were part of to allow his wife to regain her strength, planning to continue their journey when her health improved.

Fortune favoured Bannister. He arrived in town just as Elijah Jones, the owner of the general store, fell from a ladder while repairing a leak in his roof, and broke a thigh bone that took months to mend. Jones handed Bannister the clerking duties in his store, being one of the few in Brody Creek who could read, write and add. It was a decision that Elijah Jones never regretted, and an opportunity that Jack Bannister made the most of, turning the small store into an emporium with a combination of astute decisions and innovative ideas.

His friendship with Elijah grew stronger, until Jones virtually adopted Bannister as his son. Jones had no family, and time drew the two men closer together until they were virtually kin. Two years later, when Elijah keeled over with a heart attack, Bannister learned the full extent of the esteem in which the store owner held him when, in his Will, he left the Jones Emporium lock, stock and barrel to him.

Brody Creek by now, with word of the bargains to be found at Jones's Emporium had regular wagon trains coming through and a town that had been about to fade off the map was beginning to look to the future. Everyone in Brody Creek paid tribute to Jack Bannister, knowing that it was his hard work and enterprising ways that had given hope back to the town.

Bannister's face set in grim lines, and his soulless grey eyes iced over as the memories that had haunted his nights and days came to mind again; particularly the memory of the day that his life had been snatched from him.

* * *

'You polish that damn window any more, Jack, and it'll blind God in heaven,' Sheriff John Drew chuckled as he strolled along the boardwalk from the law office, pulling on a clay pipe that never seemed to put up smoke. 'Mornin', Elizabeth,' the lawman greeted, and twirled Catherine Bannister's plaits as he paused to chat. 'I do declare that this is a heaven-sent day, ain't it?'

'For those with nothing to do, maybe,' Elizabeth humorously chided Drew.

Though John Drew was a dear friend, Jack Bannister regretted Brody Creek's having to appoint a peace-keeper. When he'd arrived in town, there had been no call for a lawman; it was a sleepy-nothing-ever-happens place. The need six months before to appoint a sheriff was a double-edged sword. It showed on the one hand that Brody Creek was on the map, while on the other it was an admission of the trouble that came to a town with increasing commerce and prosperity. A new saloon, the Lazy Elbow, had gone up at the south end of Main. When it was built there was nothing beyond it but grit and tumbleweeds. Now, three months later, the Lazy Elbow was part of a row.

New faces were appearing in town; hunted faces, lined by wind and weather, with eyes that constantly kept looking at the trail behind them.

13

The Lazy Elbow had begun to offer delights other than liquor, and the quiet nights that Bannister had grown to like, sitting on a rocker outside the store gabbing, were slowly slipping away.

'It'll be all right, honey,' Elizabeth would reassure him when he'd frown at some ruckus spilling out of the Lazy Elbow. 'Things will settle down again. This rowdiness is just a passing phase.'

Bannister would nod in agreement, sure things would settle down, but Brody Creek was changing, and he wasn't easy with that change. He began to long for those first easy carefree days; for the kind of peace of mind and calmness of heart that had held him fast to the town. A constantly jingling till was nice music to hear, but contentment in a man's heart and soul were important too, and very important to Jack Bannister.

For Bannister the pain of that awful day was still as knife-sharp in his heart as it was back then. The pictures run in front of his eyes. He is back on the porch of the now Bannister General Emporium. Over John Drew's beefy shoulders he is watching four riders amble along Main. Strangers. Their horses are dusty and jaded, ill-treated and trail-weary. The hooded eyes of the blond rider bringing up the rear drift his way, lock brazenly with his for a second, before gliding on to Elizabeth, attracted by her laughter, as her banter with Drew continues. The stranger's tongue flicks dry, cracked lips, and the thoughts in his head show in his eyes, as his perusal of Elizabeth continues. Bannister wants to rip the dirty thoughts from the stranger's mind.

The riders stop outside the Mercantile Bank, opened the same day as the Lazy Elbow. The rider glances back and smiles a snake smile.

Drew asks Elizabeth: 'What's got Jack's attention, huh?' John Drew turns to follow Bannister's line of sight. His smile fades, and a frown clouds his face. He says: 'Them fellas don't look to me like the banking kind, Jack?'

15

Bannister doesn't answer. There's no need to.

'Best see what them hobos are up to?'

Bannister watches as John Drew crosses Main and climbs the steps to the bank. He waits. His heart is still. He can sense evil. Then the bank window explodes outwards and Drew is blown through it, in the same second that a gun flashes. The four strangers charge through the bank door. Rannies from a local ranch, leaving the Lazy Elbow to make their way out of town, react quickly. Guns explode. Lead zings along Main. Two of the rannies cry out and go down. Bannister shoves Elizabeth and Catherine inside the store. He feels a thump in his right side and hears the gut-wrenching crack of a rib. The bullet spins him around and off the boardwalk. Elizabeth comes running from the store, screaming. He's too weak to get off the ground as she tries to help him up. The blond rider with the dirty mind has his arm around Elizabeth's waist, and he is dragging her with him to his horse. He forces her on to the horse with the snarled threat.

'You give me any trouble and I'll finish that man of yours off right now!'

Elizabeth is astride the horse and the stranger is wheeling and galloping off. Catherine tries to stop him. The bank robber's horse rears. Catherine stumbles. He can see the rider's sneer as he brings the horse's hoofs down on her, pounding on her savagely. Her scream eats into Bannister. He tries to get up and a second bullet shatters his shoulder. He plunges into darkness. His wail of agony follows him through the darkness.

The same wail of agony that now, five years on, filled the black hills overlooking Prosperity.

★   ★   ★

It had been a long and bloody trail that Jack Bannister had ridden since then. He had hunted and killed three of the men, Bains being the third, and any man in between who had tried to thwart his quest for vengeance. His search was now on for the fourth and final man; the man who'd kidnapped and murdered his wife and slaughtered his daughter. He was working on rumour and hearsay, going from town to town, territory to territory, and would continue until his Maker marked his day, or he found and killed Luke Birch, the last man of the Skaggs gang responsible for the carnage at Brody Creek.

He'd followed a lot of false trails and spurious stories in his hunt for the gang, but had caught up with Rick Skaggs on a Mississippi gambling boat, his brother Luther in a New Orleans cathouse, and now Frank Bains in Prosperity, Montana. Various stories and half-truths had put Birch in Arizona, Wyoming, up near the Canadian border ... A hundred different places; each one he'd try. It was a big country, but he'd search every inch of it for as long as it took to find and kill Luke Birch.

Bannister's need to hold body and soul together meant that his pursuit of the gang was interrupted by spells of cow-punching, freighting, clerking, stage-driving and a stint as an actor in a travelling show. Always, as soon as his poke was replenished, he hit the trail again on his dogged pursuit. Such an interruption was now on the cards. Winter was in the air; he was tired, and it was a long trek to Arizona Territory, his next port of call in his search for Birch.

As he arrived in Hope Wells, forty miles east of Prosperity, and every bit as scruffy and dejected, Jack Bannister was not very hopeful of finding work to tide him over the worst of the winter.

3

Through the law office window, Marshal Ben Archer watched the approaching rider draw near, head down. His six-foot frame hunched against the driving snow made his face a mystery. Hair as black as a raven's wing curled from under his tightly pulled-down hat. His gait was one of total indifference, but the marshal sensed his eyes; watching. Archer let his tired blue eyes drift with the stranger along Main, paying particular attention to the low-slung Peacemaker, thonged to the newcomer's right thigh, and the loose-limbed readiness of the gunfighter still discernible even in his crouched form.

Trouble? Archer speculated

Archer's left fingers smoothed his iron-grey moustache while he flexed his right hand, grimacing at the tightness of joints and knuckles that would soon make his hands useless in a profession where speed of hand was the difference between a man living and dying. He examined his gnarled hands and swore. 'Too many damn freezing winters!'

Hope Wells was a town like the other one-dog stops strung out across the mountains, started on a rumour of riches in the hills, and finished off by another rumour of greater riches elsewhere. Towns founded on lies, and dying on reality. Strangers drifted through from time to time, and some, like the man lounging in his jail awaiting the arrival of a US marshal and a noose for the murder of a Wyoming lawman, came looking for trouble. Up to now he'd been lucky enough to make the right moves at the right time, and the men he'd planted or jailed, like Jed Lacey, his present guest, had been dumb sons of bitches, but he had a feeling that the new arrival was not dumb, whatever about being a son of a bitch.

'Marshal!'

Archer snarled. 'What do you want, Lacey?'

'For you to open the door and let some of that heat from that pot-bellied stove drift this way, before I turn blue.'

Archer chuckled. 'Don't give me notions, Lacey. Letting you freeze to death in there is better than standing around while the US marshal slings a rope for you.'

Now it was Lacey's turn to laugh. 'Ain't goin' to happen, old man. My Uncle Josiah is on his way.'

'Isn't going to make any difference,' Archer chanted, sounding more confident than he felt by a long shot. 'You'll be worm bait before he gets here.'

'Oh, it'll make a difference all right, Marshal,' the prisoner snorted. 'The diff'rence being that it'll be you swingin' on that rope 'stead of me.'

Archer scoffingly dismissed Lacey's prediction, but deep inside his gut there was a burning ball of apprehension, because he knew that once the Claver outfit put in an appearance, the killer's doom-laden forecast could easily come to pass. If Stan Benton, the US marshal, a week overdue, did not show soon to oversee Jed Lacey's hanging, his future would be about as healthy as a winter weed's.

The lawman's worried frown deepened. What if the Claver gang had sent an agent ahead? He knew the Clavers; Josiah, the gang elder and leader; then there were Ike and his younger brother Dan, each one meaner than the other, and cunning like a fox. The mountains were their natural environment, and over the years Hope Wells had been a regular resting place. They had done no mayhem in his town, so Ben Archer had left well enough alone, until the week before when Jed Lacey's visit coincided with a request for his arrest for busting out of jail, where he was awaiting sentence to be carried out for the murder of Sheriff Hank Britton, a Wyoming peace officer, and long time friend of Archer's.

Jed Lacey wasn't actual kin of the Clavers', but having hooked up with the gang the year before Josiah had taken a shine to him, impressed, folk said, by his mean and ruthless nature. It was a mutual attraction; Lacey, too, was taken by Josiah's murderous instincts. So Josiah Claver became Lacey's adopted uncle and protector.

Then there was Becky Todd, who was as hot as a cat in heat for Lacey, and would slit any man's throat who was a threat to him, and any woman's who cuddled up to him. Becky was the bastard daughter of a man who rode with the Claver gang. Josiah had taken her under his wing when she was twelve years old, when her father had been shot in a bank hold-up. The clan saw women as only having one purpose for existing, feeding them and pleasuring them, and Becky had done both. Ben Archer had seen prettier horse-rumps than Becky Todd, but when the Lacey brood got the urge, they'd crawl into bed with a rattler.

The marshal of Hope Wells decided on getting a closer look at the stranger. Catching sight of Archer donning his fox-pelt coat, Lacey enquired:

'Where're you takin' yerself off to, Marshal?'

Archer sneered back. 'Thought I'd buy me a new rope, Lacey.'

Fear haunted the killer's eyes. 'New rope?'

'Yeah,' Archer drawled, enjoying the sight of his prisoner cringing. 'Wouldn't want that old one I've got snapping. Because, boy, I aim to let you swing in the breeze until every scavenging mongrel and mountain cat has had his fill, and you're nothing but rattling bones.'

The marshal's gaze frosted over.

'That's all that any man who cut Hank Britton's throat deserves.'

Archer left Lacey whining. On reaching the snow-piled boardwalk, the marshal watched with trenchant features as Jack Bannister stomped his feet and clapped his hands to coax circulation back into numbed limbs.

Feeling the burn of Ben Archer's gaze, the man known as Gunhawk let his bleak grey eyes drift slowly the marshal's way. His frost-laden eyebrows gave him a furry vision of the badge toter, but he saw no threat in his stance. In Western towns strangers gave rise to curiosity; particularly lawman curiosity. If their positions were reversed, he'd be doing exactly the same.

The country he was riding was hard country, full of threat, and the men who rode it and risked its hundred and one dangers, from avalanches, snow-drifts, marrow-chilling cold, terrain that seemed firm but could slide away in powder under a man's horse to pitch him into a ravine or gully, predators, two- and four-legged, were men who had a grim purpose, such as he, or men who didn't want to be found and welcomed the safety that the desolate country offered them.

Desperate men. Dangerous men. Men whose nature was as wild, mean and unpredictable as the beasts they shared the mountains with.

Bannister touched his hat to the marshal in a friendly gesture. The lawman did not return his greeting. It was not Archer's intention to be unfriendly, his lack of response was down to his total interest in the stranger's flintlike features; a visage hardened by cold, wind and sun, but more so, the marshal reckoned, by the raw anger in his eyes.

'It's your damn choice, fella,' Bannister mumbled, as he slipped and slid across the street to the Wagon Wheel saloon. Knowing the marshal's eyes never left him for a second, it came as no surprise when, five minutes later, Ben Archer bellied up to the bar alongside him. Gunhawk offered no hospitality and poured only a single shot from the bottle of whiskey in front of him. He waited. The lawman had questions he wanted to ask. Bannister let him pick his own time. Another five minutes dragged by before the marshal did his asking.

'Come far?'

Jack Bannister shrugged. 'What's far, Marshal?'

Archer's eyes locked with Bannister's. 'Heard a tone like yours once before. A gambler I planted. From down Kansas way.'

'You've got a good ear, Marshal,' Gunhawk complimented. 'Wichita.'

Another minute crawled by in which Archer's eyes honed in on the well-cared-for Peacemaker hugging Bannister's hip, before he asked his next question, and voiced an opinion. 'Got a handle, mister? That pistol looks like an often used gun.'

'I don't deny it's barked a time or two, Marshal. The name's Jack Bannister.'

The name had an icy finger running down Archer's spine. He was standing inches away from the man whose fast draw and bloody trail had earned him the sobriquet of Gunhawk. He knew Bannister's story. Word of the Skagg gang's atrocity at Brody Creek was often spoken of. As a man, Archer secretly admired his determination to hunt down the killers who had murdered his family, but as a sworn peace officer he'd have to utter his condemnation of his killing spree, that allowed no man to stand between him and his mission of retribution. Story had it that he was a fair man, never killing needlessly. Archer wasn't going to show it, but in the brief few minutes he'd spent in the man's company, he was getting an inkling of a liking for him, and had concluded that he was too clean a fella to lie down with filth like the Clavers.

Bannister, too, was getting to like the ruddy-faced, wrong side of fifty lawman, so he set his mind at ease.

'I'm not aiming to stir any trouble, Marshal. I was figuring that I might find work around here to replenish my poke while waiting out the winter, before moving on again as soon as the thaw comes.'

'Where to?'

'Arizona Territory.'

'Still looking for Frank Bains and Luke Birch, huh? I hear you planted the Skaggs brothers.'

'Luke Birch only. Bains I planted in Prosperity.'

'And what did that old warhorse Nathan Jube have to say about that?'

'He showed, poked a shotgun my way . . . ' Ben Archer knew that the next couple of words from Bannister's mouth were going to make a heap of difference in his attitude to the man known as Gunhawk. 'Then he listened to good sense, Marshal.'

Archer let the breath he was holding go.

'Used to be greased lightning with an iron, old Nathan. Before a cheating woman and rot-gut used up his pride.' His eyes were sad pools of memory, then swiftly changed to a fiery anger. 'Being a lawman is the most useless job a man can do! You spend your young days hunting and chasing, and your old

30

ones skulking and hiding in towns like Prosperity and Hope Wells!' His anger turned to rage. 'Watching and waiting for the man who'll come to kill you.'

Bannister noted the marshal's flexing of his knotted fingers.

'I'd have you figured as a man who'd neither skulk nor hide, Marshal,' he complimented sincerely.

Archer considered Gunhawk for a long moment, showing a bland face, but he could not hide his pleasure at Bannister's genuine compliment; his blue eyes smiled.

'How long are you going to go on looking for?'

'For as long as it takes,' Bannister said grimly.

'Birch in Arizona Territory?'

'So the story goes, Marshal. He could really be anywhere. Depending on who's doing the telling.'

'Another week and the passes will be closed by snowdrifts; the trails too,' Archer advised.

'That's why I've got to find a job

now, or make tracks right after some shut-eye. You know of any work around here, Marshal?'

The marshal shook his head. 'There's nothing in these parts until the spring.' He snorted. 'Isn't much then either.' He glanced through the saloon window at the thickening snow. 'This is hunkering-down time around here, Bannister.'

'Then I guess it's the trail for me come morning.'

'Don't see that you have any other choice,' Archer said.

Bannister slid the bottle of whiskey the lawman's way. 'Might as well empty this, I guess.'

'I guess.' Ben Archer's smile was log-fire warm.

Two men, strangers to Archer, were blown through the saloon door by the gusting wind. The snow piled in behind them.

'Shut that damn door,' the barkeep groused.

'No need for an unfriendly tone,

friend,' the taller of the duo, a gangly man with an acid face, returned. 'Ain't no other way in here 'cept through the damn door!'

The second half of the partnership was so full of head lice that his hat had a life of its own. He also gave a lot of attention to his crotch and armpits, and a weeping sore behind his right ear offered nourishment to the lice.

Ben Archer turned his attention to the new arrivals. Bannister noted the tightening of the lawman's features. His full lips narrowed to a slit. He reckoned that the marshal was carrying the kind of worry that burned a hole right through a man's gut.

Understandable, with hands crimping the way his were.

On seeing the glint of lamplight on the star pinned to Archer's chest, the men sought the darkest corner of the saloon.

'What business have you fellas in Hope Wells?' Archer quizzed the latest arrivals.

Acid-face brazenly flung back: 'A man might want to keep his business to hisself, Marshal.'

The lawman stiffened. 'State your name and your business or hit the trail!'

'Ned Walsh,' he supplied grudgingly.

'Me and Ned was up in the hills, scrapin' for leavin's,' the second man volunteered. He sniggered. 'But I got as much gold in my ass as is in them left-over holes.'

'Ain't no law agin a coupla fellas scrapin', now is there, Marshal?' Walsh drawled insolently.

'Your monicker?' Archer enquired of the second man.

'Lute Granger, Marshal.'

'Where're you boys headed?'

'Ain't much movin' a man can do, this time o' year.' Walsh turned to his partner. 'Mebbe we'll winter right here, Lute?'

'As mountain towns go, I guess it's no worse or better,' Granger concluded, his ratty eyes settling on Jack Bannister. 'Ain't that so, Deputy?'

'I'm not law,' Gunhawk confirmed.

There was a visible relaxing of muscles in both men.

'Is that it?' Walsh aggressively asked Ben Archer.

'As it stands,' the lawman replied.

'Bring a bottle,' the acid-faced one ordered the barkeep.

Bannister continued to share the bottle with Archer until it was clear glass, then he asked the barkeep, 'Have you got a room free?'

The barkeep laughed wheezily. 'Shit, mister. We've got every room free, if you can stand the dust?'

'The name's Ben Archer,' the marshal introduced himself, before Jack Bannister headed upstairs. The marshal left the saloon under the new arrivals' malicious scrutiny, and fought the ice-laden wind back to the law office, not even noticing its intensifying chill. He was much too busy chewing on a thought that had come to mind.

'It's darnwell the craziest thing you've ever come up with, Ben Archer!'

he was mumbling, as he entered the law office.

'I'm freezin' in here,' Jed Lacey moaned. 'And my gut's rumblin' with the hunger.'

Out of Lacey's sight, Archer mischievously took a brand new rope he had in his desk drawer and casually hung the lariat on the hook of the door leading to the cells, taking delight in Lacey's wide-eyed response.

'Don't know if it's worth feeding you,' he pondered, scratching his lantern jaw.

'You gotta wait for the US marshal to make my hangin' legal, Archer,' Lacey whined.

'Don't know if that gent will make it before the blizzards do their worst. And I'm not planning on listening to your whining all winter.'

'I'll stop my whinin', then,' the killer hastily volunteered.

Archer shook his head, thoughtfully fingering the rope.

'I'm sure anxious to test this new

rope.' He chuckled as Jed Lacey's blood dropped into his boots. Though he'd set out to rattle Lacey, his own fears about the overdue US marshal were very real. Lacey's partner had left to find the Clavers when the killer had been jailed. That was over a week ago, and knowing the Clavers' haunts, he must have cut their trail by now, and probably long ago. From the second he'd ridden out, it had been a race between them and the US marshal. And the worrying thing for Archer was that he had no way of knowing who was winning that race.

His mind drifted back to the thought that had so preoccupied him when leaving the Wagon Wheel.

'Mebbe it ain't that crazy an idea after all,' he muttered.

4

On reaching his room, Bannister was pleasantly surprised by its warmth, benefiting as it did from the wafting heat of the pot-bellied stove directly underneath in the saloon. Tiredness quickly overtook him, and he lay on the bed, letting the sweeping snow outside the window lull him. Not a killing man by nature, the deed always set him adrift in a weary gloom. Frank Bains had deserved to die for his heinous crime, but Bannister would have preferred that, that day five years ago, the Skaggs gang had given Brody Creek a wide berth. Their visit had robbed him of his life and happiness, and revenge had probably damned his immortal soul. At least sometimes the hollow hole inside him made it feel that way.

He slept, and when he woke night

had settled in and the howling wind filled it with the wailing of demons. He hadn't eaten since the day before and his belly was scraping his backbone. Earlier, he'd seen the swill that the saloon barkeep had served up, and he had his qualms about eating the pigsty fare but now the gnawing in his gut was so sharp, even the excuse for food that the Wagon Wheel offered was, if not appetizing, certainly preferable to starving.

He strolled to the window and opened it to inhale the snow-fresh air, to clear away the throbbing headache that the saloon's rot-gut had given him. The wind had died to a whisper, and the snow drifted gently down, instead of swirling in its normal gusting pattern. He was about to turn away from the window when he spotted the duo who had spun Archer the hairy yarn about scraping for gold in the hills, huddled together on the boardwalk, near the marshal's office. The acid-faced one, Walsh, was carrying a canvas sack with, judging by its shape, something round inside it. He was curious, but told himself; None of your business, Bannister, and headed for the door.

Downstairs, as he gagged on the pigswill the saloon passed off as grub, Walsh and Granger, in high spirits, came into the saloon sharing, it looked like, the joke of the century. Bannister noticed the fresh slate-grey mud on their boots. His trail of revenge had, of necessity, made him an observant man. The muck in the town's streets was reddish, so the mud on the men's boots wasn't town mud. The soil on the outskirts of town, which was washed down from the many abandoned holes and tunnels in the hills was slate-grey.

His observation had curiosity value, but nothing more. Still, he wondered why Walsh and Granger had left town. It had to be mighty important business for a man to want to face into the teeth of the marrow-perishing storm, made even more evil by a pitch-black night.

And what was in the canvas sack?

The pair were in celebratory mood, calling on the other drinkers to join them at the bar.

'You too, mister,' Walsh ordered Bannister.

'Not of a mind to,' Bannister replied.

His rejection of Walsh's invitation brought a spiteful, needle-sharp reaction.

'Ain't me and my pard good 'nuff for you to sup with, huh?'

'A man's got the right to say no,' Jack Bannister answered stonily. 'I'm exercising that right.'

'That a fact,' Lute Granger snarled. 'I reckon this bastard's snubbin' you, Ned,' he stoked Walsh.

'That's the way I figure too, Lute!'

Gunhawk drew in a long tired breath. 'All I want to do fellas, is eat my grub and go back to bed. Don't plan on, nor am I inviting, any trouble.'

'Then,' Ned Walsh's stance shifted

menacingly, 'if you don't want no trouble, share my bottle. You've insulted me, mister. I'm waitin' to hear some sorry words. And if you're not of a mind to give 'em . . . ' The hardcase's hand formed a claw over the butt of his pistol.

'Sensitive sort of fella, aren't you?' Jack Bannister smiled for a second, before his face turned to stone. 'But then I don't give a shit if I insulted you; you snivelling cur!'

Walsh's cockiness slipped some. Lute Granger paled. It seemed the last thing they expected was the kind of feisty reaction that Bannister had thrown down.

Gunhawk drawled. 'Now, I know you fellas might be used to scaring folk. But I don't scare.' He stood up, kicked back his chair, and offered the caution. 'Go for that gun and your bones rest right here, mister.'

Walsh's new-found drinking partners slid away from either side of him. Even his sidekick tried to sneak away, as he saw death in the shape of Jack Bannister. Walsh's hand shot out and grabbed Granger's shirt front to hold him fast.

'You wouldn't be tryin' to back out on me, Lute, would ya?' His eyes burned holes into his cringing partner. 'We're in this together,' he growled. The lice-ridden man's Adam's apple bobbed like a cork on choppy waters, and the blood draining from his face made his skin the same colour as the mud on his boots.

'Let it go, Ned,' he fretted skittishly. 'If he don't wanna sup, it means more'n the bottle for us, don't it.'

'You takin' that bastard's side agin me?' Walsh's voice was chillier than the frost outside.

'Ain't so, Ned,' Granger whined.

'Then you stand!'

The fear in Lute Granger's eyes was raw and wild.

Walsh returned his gaze to Bannister, eyes dancing. 'You ready to accept my hospitality? Or use that gun?'

'Give it up,' Gunhawk warned. 'You're backing yourself into a hole, mister.'

Loss of face, pride and downright stupidity made Walsh scream.

'Pull iron, damn you!'

5

Gunhawk found himself in a familiar bind, not wanting to kill a man, but being prodded so that he was left with no choice. He observed: 'You have a keen wish to die, Walsh.'

The gangly man snorted. 'Mebbe it's you who'll be worm bait.'

'Don't reckon so,' Bannister sighed. 'But if you want to push this . . . '

Lute Granger, eyes suddenly wide with absolute terror, tried to tear himself free of Walsh's hold.

'Stand — you no-good bastard!' Walsh shouted. Wailing, Granger's finger shot out to point at Bannister.

'I've been tryin' to figure where I seen him afore, Ned. It was in Abilene — '

'So?' Walsh interjected, annoyed. 'Lots of folk have been in Abilene, Lute.'

'Ya don't understand, Ned,' Granger yelped. 'That's Jack Bannister you're goin' up agin.' The import of his partner's information did not register with Walsh until Granger yelled: 'The man they call Gunhawk!'

Walsh's gaze flashed back to the man he'd challenged, his eyes now every smidgen as terrified as Lute Granger's.

Bannister urged. 'Like I said. Give it up.'

Walsh dithered; his pride prodding him.

A jittery shotgun appeared over the bartop, toted by the barkeep, who was shaking more than autumn's last leaf in a gale.

'Don't want no ki-ki-killin',' the round-bellied barkeep stammered. With Bannister, he pleaded. 'Just one drink, mister, that's all. Ain't goin' to choke on it, are ya?'

For a long moment, Jack Bannister remained unyielding.

'Please, mister,' the barkeep pleaded again. 'I'm beggin'. I gotta wife and two

46

babbies, and if you fellas start spitting lead, the Lord 'lone knows who'll be leaving here feet first.'

Moved by the barkeep's plea, Bannister relented. 'Just one shot.'

Walsh sniggered, preened himself and crowed triumphantly. 'Knew you hadn't the grit for no shoot-out, Bannister.'

Lute Granger fretted. 'Ned's just lettin' off steam. Don't mean nothin'.'

Bannister, nerves taut as a bowstring, stepped up to the bar and downed the one-shot glass that the barkeep poured.

'Night, all.'

There were mumbled goodnights. The barkeep came to the end of the bar to offer his thanks as Bannister headed upstairs, and got a snarling response.

'Get away from me!'

The barkeep, stunned by Bannister's spiky reaction, stood agape.

'This isn't over by a long shot!' Bannister shunted the barkeep aside and dived to the floor, just as the shotgun that the barkeep had left on top of the bar exploded, filling every inch of the saloon's space with its raging fury. The shotgun-blast whizzed past inches over Gunhawk's head. The lower half of the stairs' balustrade was blasted away, and the hole punctured in the saloon's side wall sucked in snow. Bannister's Peacemaker flashed from leather.

Walsh, now holding a discharged and useless shotgun, dropped it and fumbled for his sixgun.

'Too late,' Bannister grated. The Peacemaker spat, and his challenger's chest caved in. The force of the blast lifted Walsh over the bar, and hurtled him against one of a pair of gilt mirrors behind the bar. The mirror shattered on the impact and speared Bannister's would-be killer with a hundred daggers of glass that stood out of his body; ugly, bloodied spikes.

His gun swung Lute Granger's way, but his finger eased back on the trigger on seeing the vermin-infested no-good cowering like a frightened rabbit.

Ben Archer came through the saloon

door, sixgun pointing, eyes switching every which way until they focused unflinchingly on Jack Bannister.

'It wasn't no fault of his, Marshal,' Granger said, eager to curry Bannister's favour. The barkeep and the imbibers agreed.

Stonily, Ben Archer groused. 'Don't matter much who started the lead-slinging. There's a man dead.' His uncompromising blue eyes clashed with Gunhawk's equally dogged grey. 'And it was your handiwork, Bannister.'

'I wasn't left with any choice,' replied Bannister, giving no quarter.

'That's how it was, sure 'nuff, Marshal,' Ned Walsh's fellow traveller again affirmed. 'My pard got a bee up his ass, 'cos this gent wouldn't drink with him. Made all the runnin'.' He nodded in Bannister's direction. 'Backed this man right up.'

Ben Archer's gaze, rife with contempt, switched to Bannister's benefactor. He snarled, 'A bit late to be a good citizen, Granger. Why didn't you rein in that no-good bastard you were in kow-tow with?'

'I surely tried, Marshal,' whined Granger. 'But Ned was on the prod and there was no staying his hand.'

Archer's humour fouled more when he thought of how he'd planned on offering Jack Bannister the deputy's job. It was a loco idea for sure. It was likely he'd use the authority of his badge to give free rein to his killing instincts.

'There's no room around here for a gunslinger!' he declared.

'I'm not a gunfighter,' Bannister intoned, his voice tight with annoyance.

The marshal ignored his objection. 'I'd be obliged if you made tracks come first light.'

Jack Bannister, though irked by Archer's condemnation, shrugged casually. 'That was my plan anyway, Marshal.'

Pointing to the corpse, the marshal ordered the barkeep: 'Put him in the backroom. If there's a break in the weather we'll plant him.'

'And if not?' the barkeep fretted.

Archer said sourly, 'Well, I guess he'll be just another bad smell to go with the ones already around here.'

'Do as the Marshal says, Johnny.'

All eyes went to the blonde on the balcony that ran in a half-moon round the saloon, Bannister's widest of all, as he took in the curvaceous figure, full breasts and a smile that could hypnotize a man.

'Obliged, Kate,' Archer said.

Kate Bonner's sea-green eyes courted Bannister's. 'It's impossible for a girl to get some shut-eye around here, with all this shootin'.' Her smile had Jack Bannister's heart thumping, and everything below that waking up. 'Who would you be, stranger?' she enquired of him.

'Name's Jack Bannister, ma'am.'

'Everyone calls me Kate.'

Bannister smiled lazily. 'Then I won't buck tradition . . . Kate.'

She came down the curving staircase

with the graceful slink of a mountain cat creeping up on a fresh meal, and paused at the end of the stairs alongside Bannister.

'Johnny.'

The barkeep paused in hauling Walsh's body towards the saloon's back room. 'He'll keep awhile.' Her finely sculpted nostrils sniffed the air. 'He can't smell much worse dead than when he was alive!' A ripple of laughter spread through the patrons. Regally, Kate Bonner strolled to the bar. 'The drinks are on me.'

Before Johnny got back behind the bar, hands had reached across and under the bartop to grab the bottles of rot-gut stored on a shelf underneath.

'A generous gesture, Kate,' Bannister opined.

'There's nothing as dampening to an imbiber's thirst as a killing, Mr Bannister.'

'Everyone calls me Jack.' He smirked.

'Then I won't buck tradition . . . Jack.' She laughed.

Bannister's eyes drifted unashamedly over Kate Bonner, while her assessment of him was equally frank and uninhibited. He quickly brushed aside his muddied thoughts as memory of his late wife came to mind. He hadn't had a woman since her cruel demise five years before, and had never felt the need up to a couple of minutes ago, when he'd looked up to the balcony and seen Kate Bonner. He felt a keen guilt now at the stirring in his groin. He'd always figured that, having lost the woman he'd loved body and soul, he'd never want a woman again.

But he was wanting now.

Kate wasn't puzzled by the sudden bleakness in Jack Bannister's eyes. She was used to seeing hurt in men's eyes. The fortune she had accumulated over the years that Hope Wells had been a wild-as-hell mining camp, had been acquired from men who hurted, in one way or another. She had provided comfort in return for dollars or gold, by making available a bevvy of beauties to bring momentary happiness to bleak lives. The heyday of the Wagon Wheel had long since passed, and she had often wondered why she stayed around. If she were fanciful she might believe in fate, and see Jack Bannister, a mighty interesting man, as the reason for her dalliance. But cathouse madams and saloon owners weren't given to believing in fate. She supposed that the real reason she had hung around Hope Wells long after good sense would have her leave was because, unpretty as it was, it was home. The Wagon Wheel wasn't much, but it was a whole lot more than the string of orphanages she had grown up in.

'Drink, Jack?' Kate invited. She led him to a table in a nook where Bannister reckoned that a whole lot of shady deals had been struck. The barkeep arrived with a bottle of finest French brandy. Lute Granger's malevolent glance in his direction had not been lost on Bannister, and he reckoned that his troubles in that quarter were not yet over and done with.

'Special occasion?' Bannister quizzed, as Kate Bonner poured the rich amber alcohol.

'Maybe,' she said.

Archer poked his head into the nook to growl: 'You remember what I told you, Bannister. Be gone at first light.' As he strode away, he issued the same warning to Granger. The lice-covered man hurried along after the marshal.

'I'm headed out right now, Marshal.'

'Now?' Archer queried.

Granger, his eyes sliding Gunhawk's way, giggled.

'Snowflakes ain't as hard or as deadly as lead, Marshal. I'll take my chances.'

Kate Bonner's heart flipped for the hundredth time since she had set eyes on Jack Bannister a few minutes before; only this time its beat was fretful, instead of joyous. It was ridiculous, but Kate knew that if Bannister were to leave now, he'd leave behind a hollow inside her. She had never been so unsettled by a man before.

'I reckon I don't have a choice,' he answered in reply to her question about leaving. 'I don't want to go head to head with Ben Archer.'

'Fear?' she enquired, surprised.

'Respect,' he replied.

Kate Bonner's sea-green eyes took in every inch of Jack Bannister before she opined: 'You don't strike me as the kind of man who'd take kindly to being booted out, Jack.'

'I haven't got a gripe with Archer. Don't see any point in making one.'

Kate's eyes travelled to Bannister's tied-down Peacemaker. He easily read her thoughts, because he'd seen that look before on a hundred other faces.

'I'm not a gunslinger, Kate.'

'Didn't ask if you were.'

'Yes, you did. You just didn't say it.'

'Sharp fella,' she chuckled musically. Then, bluntly, 'Of course some folk might not believe that, after the way you dealt with that no-good just now.'

'Don't much care what folk believe,'

Bannister replied brusquely. Though that was not strictly true. It suprised him a great deal to discover that he cared a whole lot about what Kate Bonner might think.

6

Ben Archer slumped heavily on to the Douglas chair, wearier than he ever remembered being, even more than when the town was a raw mining camp and he'd had more sleepless than sleepful nights. He stretched out his hands on the desktop and looked at the arthritic nodules on his finger joints, and knew that soon his days as a lawman would be over; at fifty-one years old they should have been over long ago, but he'd had the luck that a lawman needs to survive. Maybe at last the good fortune that he'd enjoyed was about to dry up. Not for the first time, the thought of letting Jed Lacey ride out gnawed at him. Who could blame him if he did? He was only one man, facing the murderous Claver gang. Who could argue that he should throw away his life, because that was surely what he was doing, and no one really gave a damn whether Lacey was strung up or not. Hope Wells was a town that had long since lost its self-respect, if it ever had any to begin with. He had the key to Lacey's cell in his hands. One turn of that key, and all his worries would be over. Temptation coursed through him. Angrily, he flung the keys into the far corner of the office and rebuked himself: You're a lawman, Archer! And Jed Lacey is a killer.

'Got the jitters, Marshal?' Archer pivoted about to glare at Lacey who had, unbeknown to the marshal, been watching his dilemma through the partly-open door leading to the cells. The killer coaxed: 'Ain't no one goin' to blame ya, nor care, if you open this cell door.'

'I reckon not,' Archer agreed. 'But a man can't get away from himself, and there's no harsher judge.' He began to reason dangerously that he might have been too quick to dismiss the idea of asking Jack Bannister to be his deputy.

Makes sense to fight fire with fire, dammit! he growled to himself. Bannister was a gun-slick, and what was needed to go up against Josiah Claver and his brood was a fast gun.

'Faster than a spittin' rattler, Ben,' had been one old-timer's assessment of Gunhawk's shooting skills.

'Never seen a faster gun,' was another opinion.

'Walsh was dead faster than the blink of an eye, Ben,' the barkeep had told him.

There were plenty of instances where lawmen had temporarily engaged the services of gunfighters, and indeed many gunfighters had become excellent lawmen in their own right. He needed help. So why not get the best? Of course, Bannister might not be willing to tote a badge.

'What was all the shootin' 'bout?' his prisoner quizzed.

'It's not your kin, and that's all that counts as far as you're concerned,' Archer snapped.

'Your nerves are plumb shot to shreds, Marshal,' Lacey coaxed. 'Ain't no one goin' to gripe if you let me ride.'

'Get it through your dumb skull, Lacey,' the lawman glowered. 'You're staying put until the US marshal shows.'

Jed Lacey cackled. 'You mean, if he shows, don't ya? And you'd better pray he shows soon, Archer. 'Cos if he don't, my Uncle Josiah will sure as hell plant ya. After he's skinned you alive, that is!'

'Not likely,' Archer boasted, the Devil tugging his tail. 'You ever hear of a *hombre* called Jack Bannister on your travels; known as Gunhawk? Tall, kind of skinny, funeral eyes . . . lightning fast.' He chuckled on seeing the blood drain from Lacey's face. 'Guess you have at that.'

'So, what if I have?'

Archer's foolish boast left him no way back. 'Well, now. He's going to be toting the deputy marshal's badge come tomorrow.'

'Gunhawk, sidin' with the law?' the

killer scoffed, but the worry that had clouded his eyes when Archer had mentioned Jack Bannister's name did not diminish any. 'He's a damn gunfighter — '

'He doesn't see it that way,' Archer cut in.

'He ain't loco 'nuff to saddle himself with the kinda trouble you've got, Archer.'

'Bannister needs a job to replenish his poke, so as he can hunt down the last of the Skaggs outfit. Being my deputy is all there is.'

'The last of the Skaggs outfit, you say?' Lacey asked anxiously. 'Last I heard there was two — '

'You seem to know a whole lot about the Skaggs brood,' the marshal intoned. His scrutiny of his prisoner intensified.

Lacey shrugged. 'I heard talk, that's all.'

'There was two,' the lawman confirmed. 'But Bannister blasted Frank Bains over in Prosperity, just before he arrived here. A rat with the monicker of

Luke Birch is the last. And he's looking.'

'Mebbe he'll never find him,' Lacey laughed shakily.

Archer shook his head. 'Oh, he'll find him all right. Bannister would follow this Birch hardcase into Hell.' Archer was smug. 'Having him as my back-up has thrown a real scare into you, hasn't it? That makes me really pleased.'

'Aaahh!' The killer threw himself on to his bunk. 'I ain't of no mind to listen to you talk shit, Marshal.' Lacey turned his face to the cell wall, frowning worriedly. A town and a day a long time ago rolled out in front of him; a woman too; a woman he still dreamed about nights, and still felt a surge of hot pleasure in his groin whenever he did. He'd heard of Bannister's quest for revenge, and had at first laughed at the idea of a storekeeper posing a threat to his well-being. He'd laughed less when he'd heard about Jack Bannister's tutoring by a gunfighter. When he heard of Rick Skaggs's demise on a Mississippi gambling paddler, and Luther Skaggs's blasting in a New Orleans cathouse, both dispatched by a fella whose gun left leather faster than the eye could catch; a *hombre* that folk called Gunhawk, he stopped laughing and took to worrying and jumping at shadows.

Hell, Bannister wouldn't know him now anyway, he comforted himself. He'd put on a belly, lost most of his blond mane, and the scar on his right cheek, picked up in a row over a whore in a Mex cantina, dragged his left eye askew and changed his entire appearance. The top of his right ear had been sliced clean off by an Apache knife; he'd cursed his misfortune at the time, but now saw his Apache scar as a blessing, giving his visage another welcome change.

When he'd ridden out of that shit-hole town with Bannister's wife across his saddle, he could sense the man's hellish hatred. A lot of men hated, but with time they let go of their hatred. Gunhawk's anger had grown every day since then, and there was ample evidence of that in the merciless way he'd dealt with the Skaggs and Frank Bains, and anyone who'd stood between them and him. For a man's hate to last so long, it had to be a deep festering sore that would only begin to heal when his revenge had been fully taken.

Jed Lacey's heart danced in his chest. Come morning, the new deputy would have all the time in the world to size him up. Would he sense who he was? Would some gut-feeling alert him? He'd changed his name a couple of times since Bannister had come a-hunting for the Skaggs gang, and in the meantime Josiah Claver had become his protector. Those facts relaxed him some, particularly having Claver on his side. And there were other comforts, too. As Ben Archer's prisoner, he'd have the marshal's protection until the US marshal arrived, if he arrived, to put a noose around his neck. He was fretting over nothing, he told himself. He examined his weathered and battered visage in the cell's flyblown shaving mirror and smiled. There was no chance that Jack Bannister would tumble to who he really was anyway, Luke Birch, alias Jed Lacey, were two different men. There was no way that the man who'd raped and murdered Bannister's wife and killed his daughter could be seen in the face looking back at him from the mirror.

He was settling to sleep when his heart jiggered. There was a dodger of him going the rounds showing him as he now was, and also giving a list of his aliases, along with his *real* name. His mind raced back to when Archer had caged him. He'd got the neccessary paperwork from a desk drawer chock-full of dodger posters.

Was there a dodger on him in the yellowed pile for Jack Bannister to find?

Jed Lacey began to sweat.

66

Bannister tossed and turned, sleep getting further away all the time. The bed was lumpy and the wind that had died earlier had come up again, not in a steady blow, but annoyingly gusting, whistling through the upper floors of the saloon, hammering against the thin clapboard walls and wafting through ill-fitting doors. He pulled the bed-clothes over his head to shut out the silver moonlight that was beginning to appear through fleeting clouds as the storm moved away. He even slugged from the bottle of smooth whiskey that Kate Bonner had given him from her private stock, but nothing worked, and nothing would, because his insomnia sprang from a well as old as time itself.

Lust!

He sat up in bed and surrendered his mind to thoughts of Kate Bonner. He supposed that sooner or later another woman had to spark him, but that didn't help assuage his guilt and sense of betrayal, and the memory of his wife, Elizabeth, haunted him.

Along the hall, Kate Bonner was sitting up in bed too, aghast at discovering that the immunity she thought she had built up to all men had crumbled. She was finding it mighty hard not to pay Jack Bannister a visit.

Ben Archer, also, was awake and thinking; pondering on how he'd raise with Jack Bannister the idea of his being Ben's deputy. He needed his fast gun, and he needed to save face, too, after his wild boast of already having Gunhawk as his deputy. Archer again looked at his crooked and swollen fingers. He promised himself — and this time he would go through with it — when this is over, and if you're still sucking air, you old fool, Ben Archer, you're heading to California to grow them oranges that that brother of yours has been wanting you to grow for the last twenty years.

He'd once paid his brother John and his fine wife Adeline a visit, and every winter since he'd recall the hot Californian sun on his skin, and the way it eased his muscles, and his memory would dwell pleasurably on the sight of the orange groves, and his nostrils would fill with the fruit's tangy sunset scent.

His reverie was interrupted by a thudding sound as the wind suddenly gusted. He tried to ignore the dull thumping, but being a finicky sort of man the sound scratched at his nerves, compelling him to investigate what it was that kept banging against the support beam of the sidewalk overhang, if the sound was carrying true.

He was reluctant to open the law office door, not wanting to lose the heat from the pot-bellied stove that would be sucked out the second he opened the door an inch, to be replaced by the spiteful cold that would take an age to chase from the office. Let it be, he told himself, but there was something about the sound that got into his bones to freeze their marrow.

He went back for the desk lamp before easing open the door a mite, his hand dropping to rest on the walnut butt of his .45. He'd been in too many skirmishes to have nerves, but he had them now. The door creaked like an opening coffin-lid, the oil he'd applied only a couple of days before already dried out by the biting wind.

'Someone out there?' he called, squinting into the secret darkness beyond the oil-lamp's pool of yellow light. There was no answer, just the steady thump that each second unnerved him more, as another gust of wind swept along the street. In the fitful moonlight, a shadow swung back and forth, like the shadow of a hanging man. He slid the Colt from leather and cocked it before fully opening the door, his eyes warily searching. The moon-washed street was deserted. Most Westerners were early-to-bed-early-to-rise folk, and night owling was left to men of lazy habits and useless ways.

Chiding himself, setting aside his

nerves, holding the lamp aloft, ashamed of his cowering stance, Ben Archer stepped to the edge of the boardwalk. The fickle wind had died, and with it the thumping sound. He rolled a smoke before turning to go back inside.

Ben staggered backwards, gagging. His heart tumbled dangerously as he saw the head, secured by its longish black hair to one of the overhangs' slats with a rawhide string; open, bulging eyes curiously watching him.

Archer, not a man easily shocked, fell into the street. It was a face he knew. It was the face of Stan Benton, the US marshal he was waiting for!

7

'Damn!' Jack Bannister swore, 'and just when I was about to get some shut-eye, too!' He struggled out of bed, his breath leaving him in a gush as his bare feet touched the cold floor, the saloon's pot-bellied stove underneath his room long since dead. 'Hold it down!' he griped, as the incessant hammering on his door threatened to separate it from its frame. Just before he opened the door, Bannister grinned as he imagined a frenzied Kate Bonner on the other side of the door, ready to leap on him. You're not supposed to dream when you're awake, Jack, he chided himself. He could hear that now the hall was full of chatter and shuffling feet, then screams. Bannister yanked open the door, and jumped back on seeing the suspended severed head from behind which, a second later, Ben Archer appeared, to explain in a rasping dry voice: 'It's Stan Benton, Bannister.'

'Stan Benton?' Bannister enquired at a loss.

'The US marshal I've been expecting.'

Rushing along the hall, Kate Bonner ordered: 'Get that thing out of sight, Ben!'

Archer was befuddled. Bannister dragged him into the room.

'Go back to bed,' Kate advised her girls, most of whom now depended on Kate Bonner's charity for bed and board, with callers as rare as daisies in winter. Most of the men left in Hope Wells and its environs had nothing more than lining in their pockets, or were past bedgames, and any business now conducted was on a favour and promise basis. Kate herded and shushed the women along the hall before her to their various rooms, giving support to a fair-haired girl who'd gone whiter than new milk.

'Mamie,' she instructed a woman

whose breasts were tumbling out of a hastily and carelessly donned nightgown. 'Go get a bottle. Take it to Mr Bannister's room.'

Gunhawk sat the shaky marshal in the room's only chair; rooms at the Wagon Wheel not being for sitting down in. From Archer, he took the frozen severed head, now beginning to thaw out and drip, and placed it on the slanting roof of the overhang outside the bedroom window, holding it in place for the couple of seconds that the freezing night would take to root it to the spot. The bountifully breasted Mamie arrived with the bottle of whiskey that Kate had sent her for. Archer grabbed the bottle from her and guzzled greedily.

Then he said in a rush, 'I want you as my deputy, Bannister.'

'Deputy?' Now it was Bannister's turn to guzzle. 'I'm no lawman, Ben.'

'You wouldn't be the first gunslick to tote a badge,' Archer growled, bad temperedly. 'Besides, gunfighters have changed their spots before.'

'Gunslick? Gunfighter?' Bannister questioned testily.

Equally testy, Ben Archer flung back: 'It isn't like you're saintly pure. You've killed men — '

Gunhawk interjected hotly: 'Men who deserved to die!'

Already half-tipsy from his liberal imbibing, Archer snorted. 'Hah!'

'There isn't any hah! about it,' Bannister growled.

Liquor-loosened, the Hope Wells marshal was of a mind to speak plainly.

'Handling a shooting iron the way you can took a whole lot of practise, Bannister.' Archer's jaw jutted provocatively. 'And in my book the man who takes the time to acquaint himself with a gun with the dedication and zeal that you've shown, and applies those skills in the killing way that you have . . . '

The lawman glared uncompromisingly at his host.

'Well, in my book that makes him a damn gunfighter.'

'A damn gunfighter whose killing instincts you now want to harness,' Bannister retaliated.

'In the interests of law and order, yes,' Archer argued.

'Or in the interest of saving your own skin!' Gunhawk spat.

Ben Archer flinched at Bannister's spiked but accurate assessment.

'Cut my damn tongue out, Ben,' Gunhawk growled.

'Why? You've called it right,' the lawman admitted despondently.

He held his hands out. Bannister studied the gnarled, arthritic joints, and opined bluntly, 'It takes a fool to keep a star on his shirt with hands like that.'

Archer shrugged. 'I've been a lawman all my natural. There's nothing else that I can turn my hand to, Jack.' His eyes held Gunhawk's. 'I'm eating my pride here, and it isn't sweet eating. I don't care how many men you've killed, or for what reasons. I've got trouble headed my way, and these stumps I call hands aren't going to be able to handle it.'

The marshal stood up and began to pace.

'I drifted along, figuring that I'd serve out my time here until spring, when I'd head for California to grow oranges with my younger but wiser brother.' His laugh was world-weary. 'That was six years ago. That's the way of it in the mountains. Every winter you make promises, but when the spring comes with its sweet air and balmy days it coaxes you to stay. You drift through summer until it's too late and another winter is knocking on your door, and the chance to leave is gone.' His laughter now was wearier still, as he intoned hollowly, 'But there's always next spring . . .'

His eyes filled with a sad forlornness, as he considered his crooked fingers. 'Now I guess I'm never going to grow them oranges, after all.'

Jack Bannister was not an unkindly man, and was almost lured by the marshal's tale into agreeing to accept the deputy's badge, but he steeled himself against soft-heartedness. When he spoke his tone was sharp and final.

'Sorry. Being a star-packer doesn't interest me any, Ben.'

Archer was not giving up easily. 'You came here looking for work,' he challenged. 'I'm offering, mister.'

Gunhawk countered. 'Being a lawman isn't just any old job. It's a damn vocation!'

'It'll put grub in your belly,' the marshal argued with sensible practicality, 'and fatten your poke to keep chasing Luke Birch, come the thaw.' Then with more good sense he added, 'In my time a whole lot of men headed into these mountains earlier than this, and were never heard from or seen again.'

'I figure there's time enough yet to reach the plains,' Bannister opined.

The lawman grunted. 'A man's luck would have to come from the hand of God himself to reach the plains before the passes are blocked and the trails vanish. It's damn near whiteout as it stands.' He snorted. 'So, how good do you figure your chances of getting God to listen are, Bannister?'

Ben Archer's solid, no-nonsense reasoning had Gunhawk thinking. There was a whole lot of savvy in what he was saying. While he was tossing around the arguments for and against, the marshal's impatience boiled to full steam.

'Well, then. Tell me what'll make you stay, damn it,' he wailed.

Just then the door opened and Kate Bonner entered, sending Jack Bannister's pulse skittering. He bit back the *nothing* he was about to utter. The next morning, as he pinned on the deputy marshal's emblem, he'd like to think that he was doing it to help out an old man with arthritic joints, but he wasn't that much of a hypocrite. He was honest enough to admit that the sight of Kate Bonner in a clinging black-silk nightdress, that hugged every curve and mound in her body, leaving nothing to the imagination, had played a big part in his decision to accept Ben Archer's proposition.

8

Jed Lacey's worst nightmare had come to pass; Jack Bannister was Ben Archer's deputy. As Bannister's oath of office reached the killer's ears, he slunk back into the furthest corner of his cell, where the weak winter sun had not yet reached, to skulk in the shadows and pray that the brand new deputy's scrutiny of him would be perfunctory.

But no matter how far back into the shadows he went, it was not far enough.

'Best size up your prisoner, Marshal.'

Lacey's breath caught in his throat and his heart flipped on hearing Bannister's next move; the move he dreaded most.

Archer chuckled good humouredly. 'Our prisoner, Jack. From now on that murdering bastard, Lacey, is every bit as much your responsibility as mine.'

Jed Lacey pressed back against the

wall, wishing he had the strength to push it right out. As Bannister approached the cell, his heart thumped harder than a smithy's hammer on an anvil, and a sweat more in keeping with the Florida swamps, where he'd once hid out for a spell, than the perishing hole he now found himself in, covered his body. Its globules on his skin must be sparkling brighter than diamonds reflecting light, he reckoned. He quickly rubbed his grimy shirt-sleeve across his face.

The man to whom folk had given the appellation of Gunhawk due to his prowess with an iron, came right up to the cell door, commenting to Archer, 'Shy sort of *hombre*, isn't he?'

'If he is it's something that's happened overnight,' Archer observed, and then ordered Lacey: 'Step out of the shadows to where my deputy can see your ugly dial.'

The killer's heart nearly leapt from his mouth.

'Well, c'mon!' the marshal insisted.

Lacey had no choice but to step forward. Did the sun have to break through the thin grey clouds with such brilliance right at that moment? For the first time in a lifetime of skirmishes, gunfights and dangling nooses, Jed Lacey felt that his luck might just be about to run out.

'Do I know you?' Bannister quizzed, his grey eyes boring deep into Jed Lacey.

The killer's bowels rumbled, and to his own ears sounded louder than a train going through a tunnel.

'Ain't never set eyes on you afore, mister,' he snarled. Then, forcing himself to relax, he chuckled. 'My face ain't 'zactly the kinda puss a man forgets.'

'Faces change,' Gunhawk said stonily. The prisoner cringed, and his mouth became as dry as Mojave sand as Bannister's scrutiny intensified and he offered the opinion: 'There's a whole lot of country and a mess of trouble in your face, mister.'

Jed Lacey's dread was gradually slipping away. Bannister had his suspicions, but he had not recognized him right off. The proof of that was the fact that he was still standing.

Cockily, he declared: 'Ain't denyin' I' been 'round some, and in a skirmish or two.' He now strolled confidently forward. 'I reckon you've been in one or two bust-ups yerself, Deputy?' His eyes drifted on down to the well-polished hardwood handle of Bannister's Peacemaker, resting in an equally well-polished holster. 'A man don't get to use an iron like I hear you can without trouble findin' him.' He sneered. 'Or you findin' it.'

Jed Lacey boldly stared down the new deputy.

'That sure is a nasty knife-slash,' Bannister observed.

The rat-eyed killer sniggered. 'I was humpin' a Mex whore when her husband got me from behind.' His snigger became a hyena neigh. 'If'n I hadn't at that moment got an interest in

84

kissin' somethin' other than her ugly face, the bastard's Bowie would have slit my throat.'

'It would have saved a whole lot of trouble,' Ben Archer snorted.

'Now, that ain't a charitable thing to say, Marshal,' Lacey reacted fierily, exposing the mean-minded critter behind the sociable mask he'd put on to fool Gunhawk.

The outlaw's venomous outburst got Jack Bannister's attention; Jed Lacey's evilly glittering black-pebble eyes giving the deputy a glance into his black heart, and the foulness in his damned soul. Another thing, no matter how a man's facial mien was changed by living, his eyes remained untouched, and it was in them that a man's past was to be seen.

Looking into the killer's eyes, Jack Bannister knew that somewhere he'd looked into Jed Lacey's eyes before. He could not be sure where. In his quest for vengeance, he'd looked into a lot of men's eyes. He'd ridden a lot of country in his hunt for the Skaggs gang and crossed paths with many men. He was certain that somewhere his and Lacey's trails had converged.

'Where 'bouts have you been?' Jack Bannister's question was as loaded as the low-slung Peacemaker on his right hip.

''Round,' Lacey shrugged, feigning indifference. But he reckoned that Bannister had to hear the thunder in his heart.

'I've got this feeling that we've met before.'

'Don't re-reckon so, Deputy.' Damn the catch in his voice!

Lacey silently cursed his outburst. It had rejuvenated Bannister's interest in him, just when his curiosity was abating. When the new deputy asked, 'You ever cross trails with a fella called Luke Birch?' his heart lurched dangerously, sending his senses skittering. He shook his head vehemently; his denial too animated. The killer's breath curled in his lungs and near choked him when Gunhawk enquired of

Archer: 'You got dodgers, Ben?'

'A drawerful,' the marshal confirmed. 'Sometimes it seems to me that more men are intent on breaking the law than keeping it.'

Jed Lacey's senses reeled as Archer led the way through to the office. His mood became frantic on hearing the scrape of the ill-fitting desk-drawer as the marshal opened it for his new deputy's scrutiny of its contents. Any second now Gunhawk would come marching back, and he'd be the Angel of Death come a-calling. Relief shuddered through him when Bannister asked, at the end of a lot of paper rustling: 'This the lot, Ben?'

'Yeah,' Archer confirmed. 'There was a whole lot more, but I chucked them in the stove only a couple of days ago.'

An angry Bannister stalked back to the cells.

'You ever hear of a place called Brody Creek?'

Jed Lacey's throat went desert-dry, and the ground under his feet went as shifty as Mojave sand.

'Brody Creek, huh?' he mumbled vaguely, and after a further moment's thought concluded. 'Can't say that I have, Deputy.'

Suddenly, and to Lacey's utter surprise, Bannister lost all interest. Not that the killer was complaining.

'I'd best be about what a deputy is supposed to be about, Ben,' said the newly pledged lawman.

Archer was as taken aback as his prisoner was at Gunhawk's sudden lack of interest in the killer, which had been as keen as a razor-blade up to then. The marshal, perplexed, dogged his deputy's heels. Jed Lacey sneered, and congratulated himself on having smoke-screened Bannister. With no dodger portraying his dial hanging about, he was, he reckoned, home free.

Bannister strode to the office window, lost in thought.

'Mind telling me what's going on?' Archer demanded.

Gunhawk swung around. 'He never

asked why, Ben.'

The marshal removed his hat and scratched his head.

'My marbles ain't as shiny as they used to be, Jack. So, what the hell are you spouting about?'

Bannister explained. 'When a man asks you if you've ever been to a place, like I asked Lacey just now, then you'd want to know why he was asking, wouldn't you?' Ben Archer nodded his head in agreement with his deputy's reasoning. 'So, why didn't Lacey ask?' He crossed the office to come face to face with the marshal, his face as bitter as Good Friday gall. 'Because I figure he already knew why I was doing the asking.'

Gunhawk stated emphatically: 'I think Jed Lacey and Luke Birch, the last of the Skaggs gang, and the man I'm looking for, are one and the same, Ben.' He paced the office. 'Thing is, how am I going to prove it?'

9

Jack Bannister stepped from the law office into the deserted, wind-blown street, and his breath left him in a gasp. During the night the wind had taken on a new bite that froze a man's spittle on his lips. Cheekbones burned under the whip of the easterly's spite, and fingers, if not continually flexed, soon became useless.

The night before he had helped Archer to search the town and the near hinterland for Lute Granger, having told the marshal about seeing Walsh and Granger in a huddle near the law office with a canvas sack, the rounded contents of which they now knew to have been the US marshal's severed head. Their search of Ned Walsh's belongings had yielded up a blood-stained knife, with strands of black hair, Stan Benton's colour, held fast to the blade by dried blood.

Gunhawk had never believed that Granger had ridden out, a view he'd not shared with the marshal because Archer had enough worry piling up on him. If the cur had made tracks, he'd have had little option but to sneak back into town to seek what shelter he could from the bone-snapping cold. In the livery he'd found two bearskin coats tied to Walsh's saddle; that had left Lute Granger with only a threadbare-tweed short coat to face the vile elements, and that was no protection at all.

The new-pin deputy strolled along Main, taking in the town proportions and geography, figuring that with a fight with the Clavers on the cards, such knowledge would prove invaluable. A man's knowing his fighting ground went a long way to securing victory and life and limb, too; not that there was much to Hope Wells.

The promise of gold had driven folks' ambition for a time, but the unfinished streets and debris-strewn backlots were evidence of the betrayal of the black-faced hills above the town. The ugliness that had been left behind by folk whose dreams had been shattered matched perfectly the scarred hills that had killed off those dreams.

As he went by the Wagon Wheel saloon Kate Bonner hailed him from a window of her upstairs apartment, still dressed in the clinging black-silk nightgown of the night before, which had, and now again did, send Bannister's blood surging through his veins. Sliding open the window, she called:

'Drop by for a chill-chaser when you've finished your tour, Deputy Bannister.'

He touched the brim of his hat in salute.

'My pleasure, ma'am,' he drawled.

'I'll look forward to your visit,' Kate replied, strangely coy for a woman who had made her shekels as a cathouse madam.

Strolling on, Gunhawk mumbled to

himself: 'Not as much as I will, Kate Bonner.'

At the northern end of town Bannister was running out of street, when he heard a muffled cough coming from a derelict building that had once been the town's second saloon. Untuned ears would probably have missed the barely discernible bronchial wheeze, but a man like Bannister, whose very existence had so often depended on picking up on the slightest noise or movement, didn't miss the least hint of trouble.

Without breaking stride, he walked on, his face remaining impassive, his eyes showing no interest in the rotting edifice. He walked on towards the ramshackle livery which, like the rest of the town, had dropped its expansion plans, leaving a roofless unfinished wing that swayed precariously in the wind. The walls, over all, were beginning to lean into each other for support, and pretty soon the entire structure would fold.

Bannister crossed the street at an angle, taking the risk of offering his back as a target to reinforce the idea that he had heard nothing and was unaware of the lurker's presence in the former saloon, but his every muscle was tautened, ready to deal with any threat. He assessed the risk as being about equal to that of reacting to Lute Granger, because that's who he figured it was, by bursting into the building that could hold death in a hundred and one nooks and crannies. He'd need a ton of luck to pick the right one in which to sting lead into.

He stepped on a frozen twig that cracked underfoot, bullet-like, and his heart staggered. He hoped the slight hesitation in his step had not alerted Lute Granger to his expectancy of such a happening. The next couple of seconds would tell . . .

10

Gunhawk stepped through the livery gate with sweat as thick as treacle on his body. He had only had to take fifty paces, but he had lived an eternity, waiting every second for the searing thump of a bullet in his back.

Once inside the livery, he climbed quickly to the loft, where he put his eye to a crack in the livery wall that gave him a clear view of the crumbling saloon across the street. He was counting on Granger's bronchial cough to have come from his addiction to the weed, and that his fondness for tobacco would eventually pinpoint him.

It did.

A couple of minutes later, to the right of the building's entrance, a match flared briefly before being shielded. Quickly, before Granger changed his spot, Bannister hurried from the loft, but checked the eagerness of his stride before leaving the livery. He crossed Main, careful to express no interest in the former watering hole. He checked to roll a smoke, and made a big play of trying to fire the quirly in the swirling wind. After several seemingly failed attempts, he sought the shelter of the rotting saloon porch to light his smoke. He drew deeply on the cigarette, as a man who had no cares would, express-ing no interest in the building behind him, while every second that ticked by was spent in reaching both physical and mental preparedness for the task at hand.

Peaking, he spun around, Peace-maker flashing in his mitt, and crashed through the askew doors in a fluid, athletic motion, his gun bucking to where he reckoned Granger was hiding; but his bullets only punctured the rotten saloon wall, tearing a fist-sized hole in the structure, to let in a shaft of light that highlighted him as clearly as any stage lamp.

Gunhawk knew that he was a sitting target!

A pair of bullets, with only a breath between them, ripped one half of the sagging entrance doors from its hinges, and blasted it into the street, fragmenting as it went. A third shot sent Bannister's hat whizzing skywards, and cut a track through his hair. With pain exploding inside his skull, he dived to the floor. The ramshackle saloon went into a crazy spin, while rolling thunder blotted out his hearing. Blackness, lulling and coaxing swept over Gunhawk, stealing his senses away.

Through fog-bound eyes he saw a leering Lute Granger at the top of the rickety stairs. Bannister watched helplessly as the killer slowly drew a bead on him, clearly relishing the pleasure of killing him. Gunhawk struggled to free himself from the glutinous mire dragging him under, without success. Slowly, Granger came down the stairs to stand in front of Bannister. He felt the cold steel of a Colt .45 on his forehead.

'You're going to Hell, ya bastard,' his killer gloated.

Jack Bannister both cursed and prayed. He cursed because his mission of revenge was not finished, and prayed for forgiveness for having extracted that revenge and thereby imperilling his soul.

The *click* of the Colt's hammer filled every inch of the saloon.

In that second, Bannister's keenest regret was not being around any more, just when he'd met Kate Bonner. By some crazy trick of his mind, he could smell her scent. Before he passed out, a bright soundless flash lit the gathering darkness engulfing him. Lute Granger's mouth opened in a silent scream as his chest exploded, leaving a shredded, gaping hole, filled with blood from his shattered heart. He teetered, then toppled forward to crash to the floor alongside Bannister, his eyes wildly vacant in death. Kate Bonner's face swam into view, before the darkness Jack Bannister was fighting dragged him into its swirling pool.

When he came to, he was lying on a plush, blood-red couch in Kate's sitting room. Kate was cleaning the head-wound that would, if Granger's bullet had been a fraction more accurate, have taken the top of his head clean off.

'Easy,' Kate cajoled, and gently shoved him back as he tried to stand up. His ears roared with the thunder inside his skull. 'Larry Winston's on his way,' she informed him.

'Winston?' Bannister yelped, recalling the name over the tumble-down funeral parlour that he'd passed on his way along Main.

'He cures as well as buries,' Kate smiled, amused by Gunhawk's worried frown. 'Take him or leave him, he's all we've got.'

These words were no sooner uttered than a small wispy man with spare grey hair and hollow, pallid cheeks entered the room, followed by a worried but angry Ben Archer.

'If I'm hearing right, what you did was a damn fool thing to do, Bannister, diving in on your own the way you did. You could have been the shortest-living deputy in the West!'

'And would have been, too, if it wasn't for Kate's fine shooting,' Bannister said, taking the liberty of clasping Kate Bonner's hands in his, figuring that a wounded man could get away with a whole lot more than a healthy one. Kate's warm response had him thinking that even if he weren't pole-axed, her warmth might have been every bit as glowing. Which made him a very smug, happy, and glad to be alive, *hombre*.

Larry Winston bent over Bannister to poke at his head wound, and looked more than a little disappointed at collecting a medico's, instead of an undertaker's, fee.

'Ain't nothin' to lose sleep over,' was the wispy man's opinion.

'Sure isn't, if it isn't your head,' Bannister growled.

Winston rummaged inside his black doc's bag for a jar of salve which, when opened, was more pungent than a year's supply of Mexican fly-shit.

'What's that made from?' Bannister enquired. 'Innards?'

'Larry is a herbalist, as well as an undertaker,' Kate informed Bannister. 'A carpenter and horse doctor, too. And he'll paint your house or hang your wallpaper. There isn't much that Larry can't do, or doesn't know about.'

'I'm impressed,' Bannister said drily. 'A herbalist? What the hell's a herbalist?'

'Got me this book from Boston,' the undertaker boasted proudly. 'Learned too from an old wanderin' Mescalero who put down roots in town for a spell. Indians know all about herbs and their curing secrets.'

Brushing aside Winston's arm, Bannister declared, 'Yeah. And Indians also know about how herbs and potions can kill a man.'

'Larry's been using his potions for quite a time now,' Kate Bonner scolded Bannister. 'And he's cured more than he's killed. There have been one or two accidents, but at least he buries his mistakes at a discount rate.' She smiled mischievously. 'Fair, isn't it?'

'And I throw in my best box, too,' Winston chirped enthusiastically.

Bannister wasn't in the least impressed. He leapt off the couch, grimacing at the hundred hammers beating on the inside of his skull.

'I ain't going to have no witches' brew on my scalp.'

'It'll fester,' the undertaker warned. 'And that'll be real painful.'

'It won't fester if Kate here tends to it, regular like.' He turned his gaze to Kate Bonner. 'Are you willing, Kate?'

'I guess,' she purred.

Ben Archer crooned, 'That wound could lead to a whole lot of complications that have nothing to do with your head, Jack.'

Gunhawk's smile was foxy. 'You know, Ben. I might just end up taking flowers to that hobo Granger's grave in thanksgiving.'

Kate pushed him back on to the couch and began to bathe the wound zealously, evincing a howl from Bannister.

'One hole in my skull is enough to be getting on with, woman,' he griped.

'If I'm going to nurse you, Jack Bannister,' Kate pronounced grittily, 'then you'll do as I say!'

'It could be a sweet suffering at that,' the marshal speculated.

Bannister chuckled. 'That it could be, Ben.'

Now Archer's jaunty mood deserted him.

'Trouble?' Bannister asked.

'I reckon. Art Shaw, who farms a-ways down the mountain came to visit his sick sister in town. Dropped by to tell me about seeing six riders headed this way.'

'The Claver outfit, you reckon?'

'Don't know of anyone else that'd be crazy enough to want to risk life and limb on snow-laden mountain trails, that lead to a no-consequence town like Hope Wells. Shaw says there's a woman riding with them. That would be Becky Todd, I guess.'

'Well, Ben. You've been expecting.'

'And hoping, too.' He sighed, heavy shouldered. I should have gone to grow oranges in California a long time ago.' Downcast, the marshal departed.

His attention given over to Ben Archer's predicament, before he could intervene Kate rolled him over on the couch to remove his short coat, pinning his left arm to his side. Her anger at being pitched aside sent fire racing to her cheeks; a fire that died in a deadly pallor as the stiletto blade, activated by a mechanism strapped to Bannister's arm, sliced the air inches from her face and thudded into a soft-backed chair behind her.

Picking up a trembling Kate, he showed her the clever, pressure-activated device

that a Denver locksmith had made for him by way of thanks for saving his daughter from being raped by a drunken cowpuncher. He demonstrated the mechanism for her. He slid the stiletto back into its open-ended leather sheath, then, squeezing his arm to his side, he depressed the flat disc on the mechanism to activate the spring that released the dagger, and sent it whizzing across the room to embed itself in the opposite wall. Clearly, Kate did not approve.

'Kind of sneaky, isn't it?' she spat disapprovingly.

Her hostile criticism riled him. 'It's saved my hide a time or two, Kate,' he defended. 'I don't exactly move in fine-mannered and well-bred circles.'

'I guess not,' she quietly admitted, under Bannister's frowning gaze. Then she smiled. 'I suppose that's something you could say we have in common, Jack Bannister.'

Ire spent, he took her in his arms and held her until her trembling ceased.

11

'This is as crazy as spittin' in God's eye on Judgment Day, Pa!' Ike Claver, Josiah Claver's first-born and as mean as a rattler from the cradle, griped, head down into the driving snow which buffeted the canyon trail leading to a pass that overlooked Hope Wells. 'I figure that Jed Lacey ain't worth the grief of gettin' the skin chaffed off my rump in these God a'mighty mountains!'

'Shut your mouth, Ike!' Becky Todd flared.

'Woweee!' Dan, Josiah Claver's second boy, a mite kinder of nature than Ike but not by any amount that counted for much, sniggered. 'I think Becky's got a' itch that needs scratchin', Ike.'

Ike, always ready to join in his younger brother's mischievous joshing

chided, 'Well, now. If you fellas will hold up for a spell, I'll do the scratchin', Becky.'

'Yer goin' to be a real busy gal servicing the lotta us horny bastards when this shindig is over anyways,' Dan Claver added further.

Becky glowered. 'Your pleasuring days are over.'

'You goin' to keep it all fer good old Jed now, huh?' Ike snarled, his mean eyes fired by anger, his good-natured banter gone. 'Don't know if'n me an' the boys'll take kindly to that, Becky.'

'Yeah,' grumbled a hunched-up rider with a face that would have put the run on Satan. 'Don't see why Lacey can't share what's there to be shared!'

Fierily, Becky replied, 'I don't much care what you fellas take to or don't take to. Like I said. From now on Jed Lacey is the only man gettin' in my drawers.'

'Pa?' Ike complained.

Josiah Claver drew rein, his stubbled face caked with a frost that emphasized its narrow-mouthed meanness. His dead eyes, coloured somewhere between blue and grey, settled coldly on Becky Todd.

'Due to the interest the law's got in us, we don't get to town much, Becky. Now a man can get real mean carrying somethin' fer too long that he should have left in some town whore. So you just do that what you've been doin' gal.'

'But it ain't the same, Uncle Josiah. I'm in love now, and savin' m'self for Jed.'

Josiah Claver was uncompromising. 'You do as you've been doin' Becky. Or we hightail it right now and let Archer sling that rope 'round Jed's neck, you hear?'

A black sulk sullied Becky Todd's coarse face, and a glow as hot as hell's coals fired sky-blue eyes that had given a lot of men sleepless nights, and were welcoming windows that hid a black heart.

'Ain't fair, Uncle Josiah!' she moaned.

Becky Todd, the offspring of a

one-time hellraiser who had ridden with Josiah Claver until a bank clerk had got off a lucky shot that had stopped his pump, had become Claver's unofficial niece because, like Lacey, Claver admired her rattler mean nature.

'Ain't nothin' fair in this world, Becky,' Josiah sighed. 'Things need doin' and you've the wherewithal fer doin' them, and that's an end of it!'

'Jed will be real riled,' she warned.

'No he won't,' Ike sneered. 'Nothin' will've changed. He's been sharin'. So, he'll just go on sharin' as afore.'

'And like it too,' Dan Claver's rat-trap mouth snapped. 'Or . . . ' the younger Claver's hand slid on to his pistol, leaving no need to complete his threat.

'Ain't fair,' Becky repeated sullenly. 'And it ain't right no-how neither.'

Ike Claver changed the subject of conversation. 'Why d'ya figure Walsh and Granger ain't showed, Pa?'

'Dead, most likely,' Josiah Claver replied flatly.

'This godawful weather?' a one-eyed rider called Saul Bronson asked.

'That bastard US marshal got 'em, ya figure, Pa?' Dan Claver wondered.

'Or Archer?' Ike pondered.

A galoot, name of Spike Ring, dismissed all these speculations. 'Naw. I hear Archer's hands are done for.'

Becky Todd, enthused by the speculation, joined in. 'You think Ned and Lute got to hang Benton's head outside the marshal's office as you planned, Uncle Josiah?'

Josiah Claver's grim silence urged his second son to ask, 'You gotta a feelin' in yer bones, Pa?'

'I gotta feelin',' Josiah Claver confirmed bleakly.

* * *

Ben Archer came from the Wagon Wheel saloon, his eyes peering into the latest blizzard to hit Hope Wells. Piled snow was being added to roofs that were already sagging, and, as in every

110

other winter, some would cave in. Then the folk in that house would move in with a neighbour, not having the ambition to do repairs, and come spring would move on, leaving behind another derelict building; decay adding to decay. Another couple of winters, and Archer reckoned that Hope Wells would just crumble and blow away.

He looked to the snow-covered mountains; at least they were pretty now, their scarred faces hidden beneath a clean white blanket, like a made-up jaded whore covering a face that had been coarsened by men's lust. He looked for sign of the Clavers, but his eyes were blinded by the glaring white snowfields.

He murmured: 'Anyway, the blizzard's so darn thick, a man could pass by at arm's length unnoticed.' He hugged what shelter there was on his way back to the law office. 'Perfect weather for the Clavers to come a-calling,' he sighed wearily.

Kate Bonner handed Jack Bannister a full glass of her best French brandy from her private stock.

'Get that inside you,' she ordered.

Gunhawk sipped the brandy and let it slide down his craw. The liquor was as smooth as fine silk on a woman's body; on Kate Bonner's body, he thought. He watched her move about the sitting room, and felt a stirring that he'd thought was long since dead. He'd been shot a couple of times in his quest to lay low the killers of his wife and daughter, but had never been as pleasurably nursed.

Kate went to a bureau and returned to sit in front of him with a pencil and sketch pad.

'You've got a real interesting face, Jack. Mind if I sketch you?'

'No. But before you do, mind telling me what the hell a stick of gelignite is doing sitting on top of your bureau?'

Kate chuckled. 'Gopher Sullivan, a

prospector, traded it for a last drink, just before the first snows knocked enough sense into his head to up and leave the rat's hole he'd slaved in for over two years.'

She gazed whimsically at Bannister.

'Figured that when I was ready to move on, I'd use that stick of geli to blow the Wagon Wheel to Kingdom Come. Instead of letting it go to rot with the rest of this town.'

'You planning on leaving soon, Kate?'

Her sad smile raided deep into the core of Jack Bannister's heart.

'Like 'most everyone else in these damn mountains, I've been telling myself at the onset of winter after winter that I'd up and leave come spring. But, like it or not, the Wagon Wheel and Hope Wells is home, and leaving takes a tug.' She laughed. 'A few years ago, Ben Archer and me were all set to head for California to grow them oranges he's always talking about. Then a mean-minded prospector's mule busted his leg with a kick, and before it rightly healed, winter was beckoning and we planned for the following spring. But . . . '

'How come it never happened?'

'It was a long winter, most of which was spent with Ben and me learning that him and me together was a crazy idea after all.' Her chuckle was deep and heavenly musical. 'Before winter was out, Ben had taken to feeding the mule best oats, by way of thanks for busting his leg.'

It was crazy, but no amount of reasoning could stop the rise of jealousy in Bannister, at the idea of another man cuddling up to Kate Bonner. When he spoke it showed in his tone.

'A touch long-toothed for you, wasn't he?'

'Like I told you. It was a long winter, during which a whole lot of sense took root.'

'Can't figure how you and Archer thought you'd make a pair to begin with, Kate.'

Stiffly responding to Bannister's

carping attitude, Kate declared; 'Ben Archer is a fine and decent man. And a woman could do a whole lot worse for herself than share his bed, Jack Bannister!'

Huffily, she sat on a chair opposite him. 'Now. Do you want this sketch done or not?'

Suitably admonished, he took up a foppish pose that had them both laughing.

As Kate Bonner's hand flew over the paper, he gave free rein to his thoughts, some lurid, some whimsical, and many sad to the point of tears as memory of Elizabeth and Catherine Bannister came to mind. When, after about fifteen minutes, Kate finished her sketch and showed it to him, his jaw dropped in admiration. He could have been looking at his reflection in a mirror, so accurately had she caught his visage.

'Well?' she quizzed. 'Do you like it?'

'You've got a fine talent in them hands of yours, Kate,' he genuinely opined. 'Where'd you learn to draw like this?'

She shrugged. 'There wasn't much else to do in the orphanage I was brought up in, after my drunken father drove his wagon into a ravine with my mother and brother on board.'

Bannister held the sketch up to the grey winter light. 'It's really dandy, Kate.'

'I'm glad you like it, Jack,' she murmured, cheeks flushed with pleasure.

'I surely do.'

As he studied the sketch, the beginnings of a thought crept into Gunhawk's mind.

'Can you unmake a face, too, Kate?'

'Unmake a face? Don't know what you mean.'

'Well, let's say that my face had seen a lot of country. Could you sketch me like I was before it got blemished?'

Kate shrugged uncertainly.

'Could you?' Gunhawk persisted.

'I'm not sure. Maybe.'

Bannister lay back on the couch, studying his sketch, his smile widening by the second. 'You know, Kate Bonner. You're a real handy and useful woman.'

12

The proposition that Bannister was about to make to Kate Bonner was rudely interrupted by the sound of gunfire. Through the window he could see the flash of guns, their bullets peppering the marshal's office.

'Looks like the Clavers have put in an appearance,' he said grimly.

'You can't go out there,' Kate scolded, as Bannister strapped on his gun. 'You can hardly stand upright.'

'I'm fine,' Bannister growled, though not annoyed by Kate Bonner's reprimand. He found warm comfort in its fretful plea. It had been a long time since anyone cared about his well-being. His annoyance was with the cotton wool legs he was standing on.

'A couple of minutes and you won't be able to see what the hell you'll be shooting at,' Kate continued to scold.

'Go out there now, and you'll end up in Larry Winston's back room, for sure.'

On his way to the door he kissed Kate on the cheek, his smile boyishly rogueish.

'You'll look lovely in black, honey,' he quipped.

'What makes you think I'd want to mourn you, Jack Bannister?' she flung back, her face caught between a coyish smile and a worried frown.

Bannister paused in the open door. 'Because I spark you, Kate Bonner. And you'd miss me.'

'The marshal will have less of a chance of surviving if he's got to fret about your hide as well as his own.'

He closed his eyes to force the fog from them. When he opened them again, the fog had thickened. Doggedly, Bannister cut a wavering path to the door.

'I'm not going to let Archer down, Kate.'

Angered by his rejection of her advice, Kate flared.

'A bit late to be getting all noble, isn't it?'

Bannister paused. 'What's that supposed to mean?'

'Oh, nothing,' Kate flung back, reeking with self-loathing.

Bannister reacted angrily. 'The men I've killed needed killing.'

'Don't go out there,' Kate coaxed. Then, seeing Jack Bannister's dour implacability, her anger returned. She declared, 'Dammit it! Haven't you got it through your thick skull yet that I've developed a keen hankering for you, Bannister?'

'You shouldn't have said that.' He swept her up in his arms and kissed her until his lungs hurt from lack of oxygen. 'Because just knowing that, Kate Bonner, makes it all the harder for me to walk out of here now. And if you still want me to stay . . . ?'

There was nothing that Kate wanted more, but she knew that she had to let him go. If she held him back, the man who stayed would he only half the man that Jack Bannister was now, when the shooting was over and done with. The man known as Gunhawk was a proud man, and if his pride was taken from him, he'd have lost too much to be of any use to himself or anyone else any more.

Kate kissed him lightly on the lips. 'Come back to me, Jack.'

His smile was as broad as an Irishman's on St Patrick's Day.

'I aim to, ma'am!'

Going downstairs, his eyes going every which way, he worried. I don't know what use I'm going to be to you, Marshal Archer. But here I come. As he stepped through the saloon door, Kate Bonner's image haunted him, and for the first time on the bloody trail he'd set out on, Jack Bannister wanted to unbuckle his gun and call it quits.

* * *

Ben Archer was, for the most part, shooting at shadows. The blizzard had grown thick and the wind blew it straight against the front of the law office, making it impossible most of the time to see more than a couple of feet, except when the easterly curled back on itself to sweep a hole in the storm; but even then it didn't last long enough to get a clear shot at any of the Claver outfit, lurking in the building across the street.

'You'd swear that they knew when the snow was going to part!' Archer grumbled, as more lead buzzed around him.

'You're a dead man, Archer,' Jed Lacey sniggered from his cell. 'There's at least five men out there, not counting Becky Todd,' he proudly boasted, 'and she's spunkier and meaner than the lot put together!' He coaxed: 'Mebbe if you was to throw out your gun, Marshal . . . '

'You better pray that they don't come bursting in here, Lacey. Because if they do, I'll plug you first!'

The killer laughed mockingly. 'You

ain't got it in you to do that, old man. You're a lawman, not a killer.'

Ben Archer smiled. 'But I've got a deputy who is, Lacey.' His prisoner paled. 'And he's got a really lively interest in you.'

'Archer . . . '

'That's my Uncle Josiah crowin', Marshal,' Lacey croaked.

'You hear me, Archer?'

The marshal put his eye to the glassless window, the frame having caved in after the last Claver fusillade.

'I hear you, Claver.'

'Nothin' I'd like better than to kill you, Marshal,' Josiah Claver sang back. 'But killin' a lawman can make life hellishly dif'cult for a body — '

'So,' Archer hollered back, 'are you going to ride out, Josiah?'

Claver came to stand in the middle of Main, his long coat billowing out about his scrawny frame, making him the perfect scarecrow. 'You let my adopted kin walk out of yer jail and we'll be gone pronto.'

'No deal, Claver,' Ben Archer returned, grittily determined.

'Listen to him, you old fool,' his cell guest snarled, 'and save your hide.'

'Nothing I'd like more than to oblige,' the lawman admitted. 'But this land needs men who'll stand fast, if folk are to be rid of scum like you and your buckshee uncle, Lacey.'

'You think the trash in this town gives a damn either way?' Lacey taunted.

'I reckon not,' Archer sighed sadly. 'But you see, the way I figure, if enough men stand and fight, soon there'll be no room in this land for the likes of Josiah Claver and his kind.'

'Marshal . . . '

'I've got no more to say, Claver,' the marshal called back.

'Ye're an old fool, Archer,' the gang leader shouted spitefully. 'You must have a real hankerin' to be boxed. I'm going to kill ya,' Josiah Claver promised. 'Unless you back-shoot me when I turn.'

'I'm not going to back-shoot you,

Claver,' Archer said. 'That would make me as low a skunk as you are.'

'We're comin' to get you, Jed,' Becky Todd screamed. 'And to kill that damn marshal who caged you!'

* * *

Kate Bonner watched Bannister vanish in a swirl of snow, and began to pray for the first time in a long while.

'I've got no right to be bothering You now, God. And I promise that I'll not trouble You much in the future. But if You're of a mind to help out, now's the time to do it. Amen.'

* * *

Jack Bannister's head spun and throbbed; the biting cold seeped into the bullet graze on his scalp and jangled bells inside his skull that sent wave after wave of raucous noise flooding his ears and distorting sound. Hearing was every bit as important as sight in a situation where two men could come face to face in one of the odd snow-free lulls in a blizzard. The only chance a man had of coming out on top in such an encounter was by hearing the whisper of sound that would alert him to the presence of the other man in the split second before they met in the lull.

A gun flashed, glass crashed, and a man howled. Ben Archer getting lucky? Bannister resisted the urge to fleet-foot it along to the law office. There were a hundred and one hidey-holes in the skip-and-hop distance between the saloon and the marshal's office, any one of which could be hiding a Claver or a cohort.

If Archer was hit, even dead, then he owed it to him to see that Jed Lacey still swung for the crime of murder. His personal interest in that *hombre* was keen, and since he'd had the idea that Kate Bonner's sketch had given him, it was keener still.

But first things first. Hunched against the driving snow, he quickly crossed

Main to an alley opposite the Wagon Wheel, to make his way along the backlots to the defunct store opposite the marshal's office from where, as far as he could ascertain in the poor visibility, the Claver fusillade going Archer's way was coming from.

* * *

'Did you see someone just now, Pa?' Ike Claver was craning his neck to see through the patch he'd cleared with his sleeve in the grime-caked and snowed-up store window. 'In the street near the saloon,' he elaborated.

'Dan?' Josiah questioned.

Dan Claver, who was hunkered down just inside the door and whose job it was to monitor the street but who was instead sizing up Becky Todd, lied: 'You're seein' ghosts, Ike. There ain't no one out there.'

'You sure 'bout that, boy?' the senior Claver challenged.

'Yeah. I'm sure, Pa.'

'I'd swear I saw someone,' Ike insisted.

Riled, Dan Claver jumped up to confront his elder brother. On sighting the younger Claver, Ben Archer slung a shot more in hope than certainty. For the marshal, it was a lucky shot. Unlucky for Dan Claver. The window exploded inwards. The flying shards of glass missed Josiah and his gunnies crouching low down, but Dan Claver took the full brunt of the shattered window. He howled as he danced about the rubble-strewn store, pulling wildly at the daggers of glass protruding from his face, neck and arms. It was a futile exercise, because the long sliver of glass that protruded from his right eye was already scraping his brain. With a bewildered gasp he teetered backwards.

'What's happening to me, Pa?' he screamed.

'Stay right where you are!' Josiah Claver's boot shot out to knock Ike Claver, who was leaping to his brother's help, back on his rump. 'There ain't a thing you can do!'

Two more bullets whined through the hole in the wall where the window had been, the second thumping directly into Dan Claver's heart. It was a mercy. The outlaw stood perfectly still for a moment before folding like a windless concertina to fall across Becky Todd, his blood spilling on her. She clawed frantically at him, her face frozen in horror.

Arriving from the backlots, Bannister paused in the alley alongside the Clavers' hideout, as two more shots rang out and echoed away, to let in a stillness that pulsated with evil.

Ben Archer pulled back as lead stung the inner walls of the law office. He knew that his flurry of gunfire had yielded some result, but how much of a result he could only guess at. If the spiteful hail of lead ripping chunks from his desk was a measure of his success, then it was minute; nothing more than a short-term inconvenience for the Claver gang.

Glancing through the shattered window in a brief lull, he saw Ike Claver and two other men break from what used to be Huckerby's general store. They split three ways, weaving across Main, guns blasting. Josiah Claver and Becky Todd opened up from inside the store to add their spite to the proceedings. Ben Archer was hopelessly pinned down, which allowed the three men to gain ground with no risk.

In seconds they'd be crashing through the marshal's door!

13

The man to Ike Claver's left, a one-eyed killer name of Saul Bronson, stumbled as gunfire scattered the trio. Jack Bannister's bullet had caught him in the neck and near torn his head from his shoulders as the bullet took an upwards route to exit through the top of the outlaw's skull. A crimson spout, like a whale blowing, rose from the top of the Texan's head, a split second before it shattered every which way.

Ike Claver, the quicker to react to the surprise intervention, dodged behind the second man, Spike Ring, and dragged him with him back towards the store, using the hapless Kentuckian as a shield against Gunhawk's threat. Josiah Claver and Becky Todd switched their firepower Bannister's way, forcing him to dive for the cover that an abandoned wagon offered. He rolled into a crevice formed by a busted wheel, where sheer luck would have to favour the outlaw duo, if their bullets were to find him. The problem was, his return fire would need an equal amount of favour, and if the gang decided on an all-out assault on his stronghold, the outcome would be in no doubt.

Hope Wells would be Jack Bannister's final resting place.

Ben Archer, understanding his deputy's dilemma, risked his hide to cut loose from the law office door to take some of the heat off Bannister. The brief diversion, before the gang's guns forced the marshal back inside, gave him the breathing space to break cover and scamper back into the alley alongside Huckerby's.

On reaching the safety of the alley, Gunhawk murmured, 'Thanks, Ben.'

The threat from Bannister being momentarily nullified, and hearing the hollow click of Archer's empty gun-chamber, Ike Claver was encouraged to sprint across Main, laying lead to the law office as he went, while Josiah Claver and his no-goods kept lead flying into the mouth of the alley in which Bannister had taken refuge, to prevent him from intervening again.

Kate Bonner, seeing Bannister about to risk his life by running the hail of lead peppering the mouth of the alley, and understanding the very real danger to Ben Archer, grabbed a rifle from the sitting room wall, hitched up the window and divided her fire between Ike Claver and his kin on the boardwalk outside Huckerby's. Ike Claver proved to be a dancing man, as Kate's bullets bit the dust around him, forcing him to retreat at pace, chased by her bullets back to the protection of the store.

Bannister, taking advantage of Kate's rifle skill, threw himself flat on the boardwalk at the mouth of the alley and cut loose with a pair of bullets, the first of which caught Spike Ring on the thigh, sending him crashing to the ground, howling. Josiah Claver's rifle spat in Bannister's direction. He dragged Ring inside, under a hail of lead from Ben Archer, who had taken advantage of his good fortune to reload. Kate Bonner's rifle cracked to whip the gang leader's hat off, as he dived back inside the derelict store.

'Is this whole maggot-hole of a town throwing in with Archer?' Josiah Claver ranted, falling into the store with Ring in tow. 'Becky. You go take care of that woman, you hear.'

'I surely will, Uncle Josiah.' Becky Todd vanished through the rear of the store, her grin one of evil purpose.

14

Bannister, second-guessing Josiah Claver's intentions, because there was no way he was going to let Kate Bonner pin him down from her high vantage point, clipped it along the alley to reach the rear entrance to the former Huckerby's general store, from where he reckoned Josiah Claver's messenger of death would come out.

The blizzard was lightening, and the snow was becoming patchy, forcing Bannister to approach the store's back door stealthily. The wind had taken on a fickle nature and was now blowing every which way, unexpectedly tearing holes in the snow to rob a man of his cover. He cursed freely as he saw the woman, who had to be Becky Todd, well ahead of him, dodging the debris of the backlots with the light-footedness of a ballet dancer. She disappeared into the alley directly across from the Wagon Wheel saloon, from where she would have a clear shot at Kate Bonner and, already having been on the receiving end of Becky Todd's lead-slinging, he knew only too well how gunsmart the lady was. He could still hear the crack of Kate's Winchester, and heard the whine of her bullets zinging about the front of the store. He could also hear Josiah Claver's enraged curses at being on the receiving end of Kate's firepower, a fact that gave him much pleasure. Archer too had opened up again, and between them had made life miserable for the Claver outfit.

Bannister's heart thumped in his chest at the thought that he might be about to lose the only woman who had meant anything to him since his wife died, to an assassin's bullet. His anxiety to close the ground between him and Becky Todd made him careless, and it was too late when he saw the shadow emerging from the nook that the store's dipping roof formed with the rear wall of the barely standing building.

Spike Ring, clutching his wounded thigh, maliciously grinning from ear to ear, had Bannister in his gunsights.

★   ★   ★

Once in the alley, Becky Todd crept along it inch by inch, hugging the wall, not wanting to alert Kate Bonner to her presence, and not wanting to miss the opportunity to ingratiate herself with Josiah Claver. If she succeeded in ridding him of the cathouse madam's threat, he'd be beholden to her, and likely to grant her wish for Jed Lacey to have exclusive rights. Strangely, for a man who'd kill another man on the merest whim, Josiah Claver, when owing, paid his debts.

The female hellion edged ever closer, resisting the urge to shoot until she was certain of hitting her target. Josiah and Ike Claver were returning Kate's fire as best they could, in between ducking the marshal's lead, but the angle from the store to the Wagon Wheel was too acute for them to have a chance of success without risking showing themselves; an idea that was singularly unappealing with Ben Archer directly across the street, and eager to plant them.

Their wild-aim shooting, though holding little threat, had Kate Bonner wisely popping in and out of the window, not offering herself as a target for too long, seeing no reason to chance the bad fortune of a lucky bullet among the speculative ones. This made her a difficult target for Becky Todd to get a bead on. She had to be patient. All she needed was for the saloon owner to stay steady for just long enough. She bellied down and lined up her Winchester. Becky Todd's finger pressed the rifle's trigger just to within a shade so that it needed only the barest touch to activate it.

Kate Bonner appeared in the window.

She stayed in the window, long enough.

Becky Todd grinned. Her finger applied the last smidgen of pressure on the rifle's trigger . . .

15

The next couple of seconds brought absolute chaos. Spike Ring's exploding gun in the backlots behind Becky made her involuntarily jerk her trigger finger, and the rifle bucked wildly, sending its load harmlesly into thin air. She spun around to see if there was a threat to her. The movement caught Kate Bonner's eye like a sparkling diamond in a dark room. She switched her fire into the alley, and sent a trio of bullets into the wall of the building beside which Becky Todd was crouched. A hole was punched in the wall alongside the outlaw's head, showering her with needle-sharp splinters. Howling like an injured animal, Becky dived for cover behind a tin rain barrel, cursing her jitteriness and the lost opportunity to kill Kate Bonner and gain Josiah Claver's favour.

Gunhawk had underestimated the elder Claver's cunning. As he had second-guessed his intentions, so too had the gang leader read his, and had dispatched an ambusher to intercept him. With the agility of a mountain cat, the deputy veered and leaped aside as the Claver hardcase's gun blasted. Luck was with him, and Ring's bullet only nicked the top of his left shoulder, but even so, it spun him around and pitched him into the debris of the backlot. A second, but hasty, shot whizzed past, the breeze of the bullet fanning his right cheek. He bit down and forced the pain of his chipped shoulder-bone aside, and corkscrewed back up, his Peacemaker spitting death. The Claver hardcase was lifted off his feet and flung against the store's rear wall. He went right through the decaying edifice, leaving a swath of blood behind him as he slid across the grimy floor.

Josiah Claver appeared out of the store's gloomy interior to rattle off a trio of shots at Bannister, but he'd already vanished by the time they reached where he'd been. Claver senior licked dry lips.

'This damn shindig ain't goin' the way it's supposed to!' he ranted.

Bannister covered the distance to the alley with the long-legged stride of a prize racing horse, but when he arrived Becky Todd had vanished.

'In there, Jack,' Kate Bonner hailed. 'The Pritchard house.' She pointed to the house whose tin rain barrel had offered Becky Todd cover from Kate's Winchester.

The saloon owner's words were still in the air when the door of the house was flung open to reveal Becky Todd holding a pistol to a young girl's head. She promised:

'You move a muscle, mister, and I'll blow her head clean off her shoulders!'

'Please, sir,' a man, clearly the girl's father, the facial resemblance was so strong, pleaded. 'Don't do nothing to harm my daughter. She's my only child.'

'Drop the gun!' Becky ordered Bannister.

'I do that, I'm dead, sister,' Gunhawk drawled.

'Dear God, mister,' the girl's father whined. 'Do as she says.'

Jack Bannister heaved a sigh. Much as it grated, Becky Todd held the winning hand. He dropped the Peacemaker at his feet.

'Kick it away,' she ordered. Bannister obliged. 'Harder!' The gun skidded out of reach. Becky Todd's grin was as wide as the Rio Grande. Her next order was for Kate Bonner. 'Get down here, missy. Right now.'

'No, Kate,' Bannister called.

'The same goes,' the sky-blue-eyed hellion promised. 'I'll kill the girl first, then you!'

'But you can't. Not now,' the father pleaded.

Becky's gun swept viciously across the man's face, taking most of his nose with it. Stunned, he staggered backwards, before anger hotter than Hell's flames welled up in him and he threw caution to the wind. Cutting loose with a blood-curdling howl that would have an Apache or a Sioux — and Bannister had heard both in his time — scared witless, he charged, clearly intent on tearing Becky Todd limb from limb.

'Don't, Pa,' the girl wailed. Too late to stop her father's bull-run.

For a split second Bannister thought he was going to make it, too. Becky, knocked back on her heels by a sheep turning into a wolf, almost let the man get inside her defences, but the swift reactions learned in her trade as an outlaw, taught her with religious zeal by Josiah Claver, kicked in, and her pistol barked. The man was only inches away from Becky and took the full and awful impact of the gun-blast right in the middle of his gut.

'Pa!' the girl wailed, as her father collapsed in on himself. The walls further along the hall were splattered with his spewing innards as the bullet exited through his back.

Inside the house a woman screamed.

With lightning-quick reactions, Becky Todd regained her hold on the girl, ruling out any chance for Bannister to use the stiletto up his sleeve, for fear of hitting her hostage. Figuring that diving for his gun, which Becky had had him kick a goodly distance away, would hand her the chance to round on him and likely give him the same treatment meted out to the girl's father, Bannister was left with only that gent's direct action. He sprang forward and shoulder-charged Becky, hoping that the repeated ploy would be the last thing she'd expect, after the grisly outcome of the last fracas. Becky was still goggle-eyed at Gunhawk's gall as he crashed into her, sending her spinning like a top along the hall. He was spiritedly following through, ready in his outrage to forget that Becky Todd was a woman, when Josiah Claver loomed up out of the snow, which was thickening again, to lay a rifle barrel against his spine.

'Move and you're dead, mister!' he promised Bannister. It was a promise that Gunhawk knew the gang leader would honour, if he so much as twitched.

Becky Todd untangled herself from the heap that Bannister's charge had left her in, her blue eyes blazing with an animal fury. She picked up her pistol off the floor and levelled the gun at him.

'Step aside, Uncle Josiah,' she raged.

There was one comfort for Bannister; his charge had handed the girl the chance to flee back inside the house to safety.

'Easy, gal,' Claver cautioned.

'Let me kill him now, Uncle Josiah,' she grated. 'Slowly. First his legs; then his hands . . .'

'He's tradeable goods,' the gang leader growled. 'A dead man ain't worth shit to no one.' His harsh tone softened, as a snake-oil smile showed a row of rotten teeth like dirty tomb-stones. 'You can have him, once Jed's free.'

He considered Jack Bannister, recognition in his eyes.

'Well, now. What makes a man like you throw in with the losers of Hope Wells?' His muddy eyes glanced towards Kate Bonner in the window of her sitting room. He snorted. 'Ask a silly question, huh? I sure hope she's worth dyin' for, mister?'

'I reckon she is,' Bannister said. 'Though I don't aim to.'

Josiah Claver now turned his attention to the saloon. He marched Bannister to the middle of the street and hailed.

'You in the saloon . . . Show yerself, woman . . . ' Kate had darted back inside; not to hatch any plan that would get her killed, Gunhawk hoped. Claver hollered angrily. 'I'll count to three . . . '

'Leave her out of this, Claver,' Bannister grated. 'Or so help me, if she comes to any harm, I'll take it out of your hide inch by inch.'

'Shut your mouth!' Becky Todd ordered, and whacked him on the right kneecap with her sixgun, sending shafts of pain shooting into Bannister's groin. Her eyes glowed with the pleasure his pain gave her. She quizzed Claver. 'Why should she want to come down here for him, Uncle Josiah?'

'A woman don't risk her hide like she's done unless a man is special to her, Becky,' the outlaw replied. If there was any comfort to be had from his present predicament, Bannister reckoned he'd just heard it voiced.

'If yer don't show yerself, I'll blast him right where he stands, ma'am,' Claver threatened.

'Like you said, Josiah,' Bannister reminded the gang leader. 'A dead man isn't worth shit as a trading chip.'

Claver's greasy smile widened. 'But she don't know what I'm plannin', does she now, Mr Bannister?'

Kate Bonner is no fool either, Gunhawk thought.

'Bannister?' Becky quizzed her adopted uncle. 'Jack Bannister? Gunhawk?'

'The same, Becky gal.'

Both awe and respect lit Becky Todd's sky-blue eyes.

'Saw you take out Jeb Waters and his brothers in a one-horse town on the Utah border two years back,' Claver said. 'Never saw a gun clearin' leather faster.'

Bannister grinned. 'Then you know what you're in for, Claver.'

'The Waters boys had air 'tween their ears. They should have backshot yer, and be done with it!'

He turned his attention back to the Wagon Wheel, and shouted. 'Countin', ma'am.'

'One . . . '

'Two . . . '

'Don't come out, Kate,' Bannister called out.

'I told you shush!' This time Becky Todd's gun barrel raked across Gunhawk's right cheek.

'You,' he told Todd, 'are storing up a

lot of grief, lady!'

'Thr . . .'

Kate Bonner appeared again at the upstairs window.

'Thank yer kindly, ma'am. Now yer come on down here,' Josiah Claver instructed.

'Doesn't make sense to step into a snake-pit, Kate,' Jack Bannister said.

His already tender skull became more painful still as Becky clipped him behind the ear and admonished him.

'You just can't hold your tongue, can you?'

'I'm waitin', ma'am,' Claver growled. 'And I ain't a patient man.'

'I guess I don't have a choice,' Kate told Bannister. 'I'm coming down.'

'Now that's real sensible,' the gang leader chuckled.

Bannister's mind raced. He had to do something before Kate stepped into the street, but with two primed guns on him, options were as scarce as good intentions in Hell.

Kate Bonner moved cautiously away

from the window, her hands out of sight behind her back holding the stick of gelignite that had caught Bannister's curiosity only a short time before. She edged back slowly towards the lit globeless oil-lamp on the table behind her. She glanced anxiously over her shoulder as a sudden curl of wind blew through the open window to tease and toss the lamp's naked flame. The lamp dipped, and for a desperate moment looked like dying as the wind maliciously dragged the flame with it as it crossed the room.

Time was short. She could sense Josiah Claver's growing suspicion.

'Don't wanna see my next birthday afore you get down here, ma'am,' he called out.

'I'm coming,' Kate returned sociably.

'Well, git,' Becky Todd screamed. 'Right now!'

Kate felt the heat of the lamp as she guided the gelignite fuse on to the flame, grimacing as another wisp of wind blew the flame on to her exposed wrist. The fuse fizzed, but did not take. Was it damp? It was likely, just lying on top of the bureau for weeks. She grimaced and smothered the howl of pain that welled up inside her as she steadfastly held the fuse to the flame. Relief flooded through her on hearing the fuse crackle, and she saw a shower of diamond-bright sparks fan out on either side of her.

It was a ten second fuse.

Kate began counting.

16

Ben Archer, veteran of a hundred skirmishes, knew that Josiah Claver had him over a barrel, with Bannister as his prisoner and Kate Bonner about to be added as another trading chip, and there was only one trade; Jed Lacey's freedom in return for their lives. It was a bind he had not anticipated finding himself in but experience had taught him that sometimes even the most advantageous circumstances turned against a man. He'd figured that with Jack Bannister — Gunhawk — on his side, his worries about the Claver outfit were old hat. Gunhawk was the last man he'd have reckoned on being hoodwinked.

Lute Granger's bullet must have knocked his senses for six, he murmured to himself. Pretty ironic, he thought. Bannister was going to be the agent that kept Lacey safe for a hanging rope. Now he was going to be the key to open his damn cage.

As he watched the unfolding drama, the lawman tussled with his conscience. Had he the right to make a trade that would let a killer walk free? On the other hand, had he the right to play God and throw away two lives, if he resisted Claver's demands? Because that's exactly what he would do, if he bucked the gangleader's wishes. Josiah Claver, in the blink of an eye, would not hesitate to slaughter Jack Bannister and Kate Bonner. Claver was a natural born killer, and he liked his trade.

Damn! If it were only Bannister who was in the outlaw's clutches. The West could do with one less gunfighter. Gunhawk had lived by the sword, so he couldn't gripe about dying by the sword. He had freely chosen his way of life, and could not complain when the odds stacked against him. But the West was pitifully short of fine women, and Kate Bonner fell into that category.

Ben Archer's shoulders slumped. He was kidding no one but himself. He was too fair a man and too dedicated a lawman to sacrifice any man's life, even the hide of a gunfighter. Besides, he'd have to admit to having developed a liking for Jack Bannister. Yes, to all intents and purposes he was a gunfighter, but not of the mould of those critters whose eyes glowed like the Devil's coals when pulling a trigger.

'What's happenin' out there, Marshal?' Jed Lacey quizzed anxiously, worried by the lengthening silence.

Mischievously, Archer replied, 'I reckon Bannister's dispatched your kin to hell, Lacey.'

'Ain't so,' the killer screamed. 'Ain't no man Josiah Claver's equal when it comes to shootin'. The conniving kind anyway,' he boasted.

'I guess you know your buckshee uncle pretty well,' the lawman snorted.

* * *

'You comin' out or not, ma'am,' Josiah Claver hailed, his annoyance needle-point sharp.

'On my way,' Kate called back, then continued her count. ' . . . five . . . six . . . ' She rushed to the open window.

'What's that crazy woman doin' now, Uncle Josiah?' Becky Todd wondered, on seeing Kate Bonner at the window, right arm flung back, sparks buzzing around her like a saint's halo.

'Shit!' Claver hollered, and dived through the open door of the Pritchard house, slamming it shut, recognizing the sparkling stick in Kate's hand for what it was.

Gelignite!

Bannister, too, dived for cover, choosing the underside of the nearby boardwalk, hoping that the explosion would not bring the Pritchard house down on top of him. Becky Todd, gawky-eyed and confused, lost precious seconds while the gelignite was hurtling through the air. By the time the sparkling stick bounced in the mouth of the alley, it was too late to go on the leaping canter she decided on, back along the alley.

She might have had luck on her side as the geli hovered above a pool of icy water, and then bridged it to roll around the rim of a second pool, before tumbling down the natural lie of the street away from the pool and into the alley.

Becky Todd's luck ran out.

The blast, intensified by the confines of the alley, shook the buildings on either side to their foundations and beyond, showering debris down on Becky as she ran. The explosion chased her along the alley, swept her up in its fury and tossed her into the air, setting her alight. Her scream reached all the way to the pit of Hell to announce her arrival. As the explosion unfurled and vanished at the far end of the alley, it yielded up Becky Todd, torn, scorched and bloodied.

'Becky!' Jed Lacey's scream was one

of utter anguish.

The thunder of the explosion lifted over the town with the roar of an angry demon, smashing windows and doors, sending slates and a variety of debris sky-high in the vicinity of its furious origin.

Gunhawk, quickest to react, rolled from under the boardwalk, reclaimed his Peacemaker, and burst through the shattered door of the Pritchard house. The house was brooding and silent. He edged along the hall's gloomy confines, pausing to listen with every step taken. The house creaked and sighed, still settling after the gelignite blast. Shadows moved. Once or twice his gun almost spat. The trick was to pick the right moving shadow, because he'd have only one chance to square accounts with Josiah Claver, if that.

A single mistake was all it would take to send him winging to his Maker.

★　★　★

158

Kate Bonner's heart was doing a jig. She'd seen Bannister fling himself into the Pritchard house in pursuit of Josiah Claver, and each second was longer than any winter she had endured in Hope Wells. The plans she'd been pondering on since she'd set eyes on the man known as Gunhawk the night before, were now on hold. There would be only one man leaving the Pritchard house, and if that man was not Jack Bannister, the rest of her days wouldn't matter a jot.

★   ★   ★

'Stop your damn whining!' Archer shouted unsympathetically at his prisoner. 'If that woman of yours has been gathered by the Grim Reaper, it's all she deserves. She sure as hell dispatched enough his way before her.'

Jed Lacey strained like a wild animal at the cell door. 'I'm goin' to rip your heart out, Archer,' he yelled.

'Josiah . . . Becky . . . ' Ike Claver's

159

voice quaked from the edge of Huckerby's door. 'Answer me, dammit!'

'The dead can't answer you, Ike Claver,' Archer taunted from the law office window. 'Looks like you're on your own, boy.'

'Ain't so!' Claver screamed, and leaped into the store's door to sling wild angry lead the marshal's way.

'Give it up, Claver,' Ben Archer advised.

'Don't you go givin' an'thin' up. You hear me, Ike?' Lacey shouted at the top of his lungs.

'I ain't, Jed,' the outlaw shouted back, but none too convincingly.

Archer sent a slug into the store's door frame that had Ike Claver scrambling back inside, still calling out to his kin, his voice high with panic. 'Josiah . . . Becky . . . '

* * *

Jack Bannister stepped on to the threshold of the Pritchards' sitting room, and came face to face with Eve

160

Pritchard, sitting white-faced in an invalid chair, her daughter, stained with her father's blood, clutching her hands.

Josiah Claver held a cocked gun to Eve Pritchard's head.

'Step right on in, Mr Bannister,' he crooned.

'You know, Claver,' Gunhawk sighed. 'I'm getting really ticked off of you getting the drop on me.'

The outlaw sniggered. 'Now, I've got me three to trade.'

Jack Bannister let his shoulders slump despondently, and his face took on a hound-dog look.

'I guess you have at that.' He was banking on his well-acted show of despondent surrender to make the gang leader cocky.

It did.

'Slide the Peacemaker this way,' Claver instructed with the casualness of a man who thinks he's got his enemy at his mercy. 'Guess it's true that the Devil looks after his own.'

'It looks that way, sure enough,'

Bannister agreed. He laid the gun on the floor, straightened up with the weary air of a man who's run out of options, and folded his arms across his chest. While he slowly applied pressure to the mechanism up his left sleeve, he continued conversationally to allay any suspicion that Josiah Claver might have.

'You know, Claver. I've got to hand it to you. You're one clever *honcho*.' The gang leader was still basking in his own glory when Bannister's left arm shot out, his wrist curling back. The stiletto whizzed from its sheath, the blade flashing, a deadly missile that held Claver mesmerized for the second before it stuck quivering in his throat, its tip protruding from the back of his neck. The outlaw teetered about the room, desperate fingers pulling the stiletto from his throat. Blood spurted, then gushed, pouring from his mouth down his shirt-front. The gut-wrenching gurgle of his flooding lungs filled the room. He slewed sideways and crashed through the sitting room window on to the boardwalk. The shattering glass sliced his face to a bloody pulp.

Gunhawk casually strolled to the window and looked out, shaking his head.

'Thing is, Claver,' he grinned, 'you just can't trust the Devil.'

On seeing the gang-boss crash through the Pritchards' window and lie still, Ike Claver threw his gun into the street and came out, jibbering.

'Don't shoot me.'

Kate Bonner sprinted across from the saloon to fling herself into Bannister's arms. Ben Archer cut loose with an ear-shattering *yee-haah* that must have reached all the way to Texas.

★   ★   ★

Gunhawk revelled in the soft curviness of Kate Bonner in his arms. The scent of her in his nostrils kicked into play feelings that he'd not had since lying with his wife, Elizabeth. For reasons buried deep in his heart, and some right of that moment, he distanced Kate from him. She frowned, puzzled by his undoubted need for her, and yet his reluctance to take her.

He explained in a hushed tone. 'It's been a long trail, Kate, and I've got a thirst for revenge that hasn't yet been satisfied.' He heaved heavy shoulders. 'And there's been a woman who meant more to me than life itself, whose ghost still walks with me. All in all, I'm not a fitting man for you, Kate Bonner,' he concluded.

Kate stepped back, uncertain as to what she should do, but fully sure of what her feelings for Jack Bannister were telling her to do. Take him in her arms and hold him for as long as it took to make him hers. She had met a lot of men, fine and good men, but he was the only man to have lit a flame in her that would take for ever to quench.

'You know,' she said, 'next spring I really am going to move on from this damn town!'

'California?' Bannister enquired. 'Maybe grow oranges?' His gaze went Ben Archer's way, as the marshal raced along the street still *yee-haahing* at the top of his voice after putting Ike Claver in the slammer.

Kate Bonner laughed sadly.

'Maybe, Jack.'

In the midst of the back-slapping and excitement that events had stirred, Bannister was never so alone.

17

'You're what?' Archer grumbled the next morning, when Bannister told him he was moving on. 'You'd be loco to face these mountains now, with winter more than settled in.' He sloshed piping-hot coffee into Bannister's tin cup. 'Anyway, you came here looking for work to tide you over until spring. You've got it.'

'Restless feet, I guess,' Gunhawk sighed, sipping the thick-as-molasses brew that the marshal served up as coffee.

'Feet, huh?' The lawman grinned. He craned his neck to meet Bannister's eyes. 'You're the first man I know of who got restless *feet* around Kate Bonner.' His grin developed into a wry chuckle. 'If they got restless, it was a tad north from their feet that their restlessness showed.'

Archer's good-natured banter drew a smile from his deputy.

'You're nobody's fool, Marshal Archer.'

'A fella don't have to have second sight to see the sparks flying between you and Kate.' Archer rolled a smoke, letting the mood settle.

'Kate is a fine woman . . . ' Bannister began.

'Uh-huh,' the marshal agreed.

'Deserving the best a man has to give . . . ' Gunhawk said.

'Uh-huh,' Archer agreed again.

'She needs a settling kind of man . . . '

'Uh-huh.'

'Damn it, Ben! Is that all you've got to say?'

'Uh-huh,' the lawman drawled.

Jack Bannister leapt from his chair to edgily pace the office, going off at all sorts of angles, winding back on his footsteps to storm off once more, like a drunk trying to reach home.

'You're in love with Kate Bonner,' Archer stated matter-of-factly. 'And I can't say that I blame you. She's one prize woman.' He growled. 'Quit your pacing, Bannister. It's driving me loco. Sit, dammit!'

Jack Bannister uneasily seated, the marshal went on, 'And she's in love with you. Hell, it's a problem most men pray for.' His blue eyes held a thousand memories and dashed hopes. 'Thought for a spell that Kate and me would — ' He sprang out of his chair to angrily declare: 'Marry the woman, you hole-in-the-head bastard!'

'Marry?' Gunhawk groaned. 'Now who's got a hole in the head, Ben Archer? What life would she have with me?'

'Kate knows you're no saint. But it doesn't seem to matter none to her.'

Frustrated, Bannister exclaimed grimly, 'My revenge isn't over with, Ben. There's still one of the Skaggs outfit to plant.'

Equally frustrated, Archer flung back, 'No matter how many men you kill, it won't bring back the dead.' He placed fatherly hands on Gunhawk's shoulders and shook him gently. 'Leave it be, Jack. Settle down with Kate Bonner.'

Bannister slapped the gun on his hip. 'Even if I did as you suggest, Ben, there's still my wife's ghost.'

'Your wife's ghost?'

'I loved my wife like no man's ever loved a woman before or will again. Kate would always be second-best to Elizabeth; her ghost would always be there. And that isn't good enough for a woman of Kate Bonner's calibre.'

His frustration with his deputy hiking further, Archer declared harshly: 'The dead are dead! And the living must cope the best they know how to find happiness. Disturbing their spirits by refusing to let go don't do them or us any good.' He thumped his fist on the desk. 'You can't stay in love with a ghost for the rest of your natural, Jack.'

Bannister conceded the truth of the lawman's reasoning, but he found no solace in his words.

'Maybe,' he pondered, 'the ghosts

169

will leave when the final blood is spilled, Ben?'

'Not if you won't let them go, they won't,' the marshal concluded.

'I don't know if I can rest easy knowing that the last member of the Skaggs gang, Luke Birch, hasn't paid the price, Ben.'

The marshal was taken aback by the fever of his deputy's sudden and excited leap for the office door.

'Lacey!' yelled Bannister.

'Where the dev . . . ?'

Bannister wasn't paying any heed. There was no stopping him.

'What about Lacey?' the marshal called to his hastily departing deputy.

* * *

Ike Claver sidled up to the bars separating his cell from Jed Lacey's, a knowing smile on his ugly visage.

'What've you got to be grinning like a pleasured man for?' Lacey grunted sourly. 'You're joinin' me on the damn gallows, Ike Claver.'

'Ain't neither of us goin' to be rope-bait, Jed,' Ike pronounced with such cockiness that Lacey's curiosity was stirred. Ike Claver gave his fellow prisoner a foxy smile. 'You and me are walkin' free,' he promised.

'An' how're we goin' to do that, Ike?' Lacey coaxed, not sure whether Claver had taken leave of his senses. Facing a noose could do that to a man.

Ike Claver took off his hat, stained by sweat and hair that hadn't been washed in years. He undid the Stetson's band to reveal a string of rawhide, as thin and as wicked as a stiletto-blade, its length punctuated by tiny tight knots. He dangled the rawhide garrotte in front of Lacey's eyes like a hypnotist would his watch, and the effect was every bit as mesmerizing. 'This will open a man's throat as good as any damn knife I knowed,' Claver boasted.

'Guess it will at that, Ike,' Lacey enthused, his fingers feeling the taut texture of the ligature.

'Now,' Ike Claver whispered, 'all we've got to do, is get that badge-toter near 'nuff to . . . ' The outlaw looped the rawhide garrotte around his neck and gagged theatrically.

His fellow killer sniggered, the Devil's mischief animating his eyes.

'And I thought you only had air 'tween your ears, Ike.'

★   ★   ★

Jack Bannister was headed back to the Wagon Wheel saloon, leaving a startled Ben Archer filling the law office door, muttering, 'What bee's got up his ass?' On reaching the saloon, Gunhawk crashed through the door, and without breaking stride stalked across and took the stairs three steps at a time. On gaining the top of the stairs, he turned right and loped along the balcony, his pace quickening even more as he marched along the hall to rap on Kate Bonner's door.

The saloon owner's heart was kicking

harder than a bucking mule. Kate had been observing Jack Bannister's fleet-footed progress from the law office, growing more breathless by the second as his destination became clear. Now he was hammering on her door, like a man possessed.

'Open up, Kate!'

What was the urgency of his visit? she wondered, but dared not let her thoughts take flight, and yet . . .

She opened the door. Bannister burst past her into the room, dragging her with him. Kate finally let the fanciful dreams she'd been dreaming blossom, until Gunhawk grabbed her pencil and sketch pad from the bureau, and then hauled her along with him back to the marshal's office at a frenzied pace, ignoring all her questions. Arriving breathless at the marshal's office, Kate, angered by his brash treatment of her, drew up short and demanded:

'What's got you so all-fired up, Jack Bannister?'

'A fair question, Jack,' Ben Archer agreed.

There was no stopping his progress, even Archer had to give way as his deputy charged through to Jed Lacey's cell. He thrust the sketch pad and pencil into Kate Bonner's hands.

'You recall me asking you if you could draw a face like it was before it collected any blemishes, Kate?' He reached through the bars, grabbed Lacey by the shirt and hauled him forward until his face pressed against the bars.

'Like that.' He pointed to the killer's facial scar, and Lacey's bowels threatened looseness. Bannister questioned Kate. 'Can you take away five years and make this man's face look like it might have been then?'

The saloon owner was uncertain. 'I'm not sure I can, Jack. And why would you want me to do that in the first place?'

Luke Birch, alias Jed Lacey, knew why, and the knowledge nearly stopped his heart beating.

'Try, Kate,' Gunhawk demanded. His grim gaze settled on the killer. 'I reckon the outcome will make mighty interesting viewing.'

'I can try,' Kate said. 'But it will be just my imagination at work, Jack.'

'Do the best you can, Kate,' he cajoled.

Kate Bonner studied Lacey's face thoughtfully. He tried desperately to turn his face aside to stunt her view as she sketched. Bannister grabbed the killer's face and held it firm.

'You keep that sin-rotten face right where it is,' he ordered. He watched the man materializing under Kate Bonner's deft touch with increasing interest. 'Like I said,' he growled. 'Mighty interesting viewing.'

'What in tarnation is going on, Deputy?' Archer demanded to know officiously, resenting his exclusion from the proceedings.

'Be patient,' Gunhawk urged, and promised, 'You'll see.'

'I ain't feelin' so good, Marshal,' Jed Lacey whined. He broke free of Bannister's grasp, clutching his midriff, and toppled on to his bunk with his face turned to the wall. Bannister drew his pistol. When he spoke, his voice held a steely resolve.

'Stand up, Lacey. Or I'll shoot you where you lie.'

Archer and Kate Bonner looked on in astonishment at the twist of hatred that contorted Jack Bannister's features.

'I mean what I say,' he warned the prisoner.

The marshal slid his gun from leather in a tense stand-off.

'I do too, Jack. What you're proposing is cold-blooded murder, and it isn't going to happen. Not in my jail!'

'Stay out of this, Ben,' Gunhawk cautioned Archer. 'You don't understand.'

'There's nothing to understand,' the lawman flung back sternly. 'Like I said. There'll be no unlawful killing in my jail!'

Bannister considered the marshal for a long moment before sliding the Peacemaker back in its sheath. Then he delivered a solemn warning.

'If Kate's sketch comes out the way I'm expecting it to, Marshal. I damn well won't allow you or anyone else to stand in my way.' Turning to Kate, he growled, 'What're you waiting for? Get drawing.'

'Do as my deputy says,' Archer ordered Lacey. 'Let's see what the devil he's ranting on about.'

The killer's face curled in acted pain. 'I told ya, Marshal. I don't feel so good.'

'Show your face and show it now,' the lawman grated.

The minutes it took Kate to finish the sketch were some of the longest in Jack Bannister's life. There were only a few longer, and those were the minutes back in Brody Creek, five years ago, on the Devil's day when his world caved in.

'Finished?' he enquired of Kate,

when her pencil stopped. She handed him the completed sketch, and Gunhawk's face froze as hard as Arctic ice, as a face as close to that of Luke Birch as didn't matter looked back at him. A black rage welled up inside him, as the killer's foul deeds flashed before his eyes. He could hear his daughter's screams and his wife's pleading, as if by some magic, he had been transported back to Brody Creek. The awful images of finding Elizabeth's violated body two days after Birch's visit were as horrific as if he were, at that very moment, standing in the cave where the Brody Creek posse had found her, bloodied and battered, staked out like a wild animal, legs spread-eagled.

'Give him a gun!' he ordered Ben Archer.

The fear that had been threatening Jed Lacey's bowels triggered looseness, filling the narrow confines of the cells with a gut-wrenching stench.

'I don't want no gun,' he screamed.

'Give him a gun,' Bannister again

ordered the marshal. Archer had to fight off his deputy's attempts to grab his gun. 'That's Luke Birch, the last man standing of the Skaggs gang, Ben.'

'Leave him be, Jack,' Kate Bonner pleaded. 'Let the hangman do his work.'

'You stay out of this, Kate,' he snapped. 'You've done what you came to do.' He grabbed her arm and frog-marched her to the door. 'Now go!'

'That's all you can think of, isn't it?' Kate Bonner flared. 'Killing and more killing.' She shook her head sadly. 'You've got a killing lust, Jack. You're wearing the mark of Cain.'

Staggered somewhat by her fiery rebuke, Gunhawk pleaded, 'This is the end of the line, Kate. Birch is the last of the Skaggs brood.'

Kate looked at him with a tired sadness. 'I guess you're a no-good gunfighter, after all, Jack Bannister. Dressed up to look like an Avenging Angel.'

Bannister growled. 'If that's the way

you feel there's nothing more to be said, Kate.'

'I guess there isn't at that,' she murmured.

He watched her sashay along the boardwalk to the Wagon Wheel with feelings that were tumbling, one into the other, and the end result was an addled brain. Kate Bonner's words taunted his ears. *I guess you're a no-good gunfighter, after all* . . . Was it true? Would he be able to hang up his gun after killing Luke Birch? Or had its evil power ensnared him for ever? He had heard of men who had fallen prey to the lure of a smoking gun.

To hell with Kate Bonner! Birch was going to pay his full dues for his heinous crime, and the price was his life. He turned back into the marshal's office to find Ben Archer grimly standing firm.

'Don't stand in my way, Ben,' he warned the lawman. 'I'm not of a mind to kill you. But if I have to, I will,' he finished resolutely.

18

'You know,' Ben Archer drawled, 'I reckon that Kate Bonner's got you right, Bannister. I've known men who started out, just like you, righting wrongs. Then, their work over and done with, they came up with a whole passel of reasons to keep on packing a gun and killing — '

Bannister intejected: 'I told Kate, now I'm telling you.' His hand angrily slapped the Peacemaker on his hip. 'This iron is out the window when Birch bites dust.' Grimly, he pronounced: 'An eye for an eye, Ben. That's fair.'

'Killing never solved a damn thing,' the marshal countered. 'Blood borrows blood, Jack.' He shifted his stance. 'And someone has to take a stand.'

Gunhawk scoffed. 'You're no way near being fast enough, Ben.'

Archer shrugged. 'Maybe I'll get lucky.'

'You'll get dead!'

'There's a whole mess of different ways to die. Some men are still breathing, but dead anyway.' His eyes clashed with Jack Bannister's. 'Poisoned by hatred. Unable to feel, forgive, forget . . . or love.'

'A philosophizing lawman,' Gunhawk snorted. 'Ain't that something to behold?' His sarcastic remark was at odds with what he was feeling inside. There was a lot of truth in what Ben Archer had said.

'Would Elizabeth or Catherine have wanted all this killing done in their names?' the marshal speculated.

Bannister said quietly, 'Their ways were as gentle as a summer breeze.'

Ben Archer placed his gun on the desk and stepped aside, leaving the way clear to the cells. Gunhawk took a couple of steps forward, and then came up short. He took off his deputy's badge and placed it on the desk alongside the marshal's gun.

'You see that that bastard hangs high, Ben.'

'I will,' promised Archer.

Bannister swung around and was out of the door before the temptation teasing at him changed his mind. He saw Kate Bonner watching from her sitting room window. She smiled, the relief on her face as visible as a lamp in the belly of a mine.

★ ★ ★

'What's the badge-toter so all hell fired up 'bout you fer, Jed?' Ike Claver enquired, able to breathe again now that the threat of gunplay had receded.

Lacey ignored Claver's curiosity. 'We've got to vamoose outa this place fast, Ike. Give me that damn rawhide necklace.'

Claver passed the garrotte over. His fellow prisoner went to lie down on his bunk, curled up, and let loose with a howl that had Claver cringing.

183

'Marshal . . . Marshal, you hear me?' Lacey called.

A disgruntled Archer made an appearance.

'It's likely the whole damn territory heard you, Lacey.'

'I gotta have a doc,' the killer groaned, clutching his belly.

'We haven't got a sawbones,' the marshal informed him. 'Only an undertaker who doubles as one. And almost everything else to boot.'

'He'll do,' Lacey whined. He let out an even keener howl, shot upright, went stiff, rolled his eyes and collapsed back on his bunk to lie perfectly rigid.

Ike Claver reached through the bars to touch him, and offered a diagnosis.

'Shit. I think he's dead, Marshal.'

The ruse worked. Archer, a caring man, even to those who didn't deserve caring for, opened the cell door.

'Take his pulse,' Ike Claver encouraged Archer, and hid his sly smile behind his hand as the lawman bent over Jed Lacey.

★ ★ ★

Kate Bonner soulfully considered Jack Bannister, and speculated: 'If you're through with killing, Jack, maybe you're also through with trail-wandering?'

'Kate Bonner,' he said, 'it wouldn't take a whole lot of persuading to keep me here with you. But I'm not the man to make you happy.'

Kate replied logically, 'How do you know, until you try?'

He shook his head. 'You'd be living with ghosts, Kate. Of the men I've killed, and the woman I loved. You deserve a man who's only got time for you.'

'When you walked out of the marshal's office just now, the healing began. In time the ghosts will leave, too, I reckon.'

Bannister's doubts were not assuaged, and he concluded with finality, 'I love you too much to make you unhappy, Kate.'

She came to him and took his hands

in hers. She drew him with her to the bedroom. 'If you have to go, Jack Bannister,' she purred, 'leave me a memory for my old age.'

* * *

Ben Archer found a strong pulse beating in Jed Lacey, but realized much too late that he'd been fooled like a first-day greenhorn. Lacey's fist came up with shoulder-jarring force in the marshal's gut. As Archer doubled over, the killer sprang from the bunk, looped the rawhide garrotte around his neck, and expertly twirled its ends together to tighten and tighten the deadly noose, until Archer's eyes were ready to pop. The ligature began to draw blood as it cut into the marshal's throat.

Mustering what little energy he had left after Lacey's hammer-blow, Archer bucked and kicked out, slamming the killer back against the dividing bars between his and Ike Claver's cages. The killer's wind left in a gush of foul breath, and the marshal felt a slight slackening of the noose. He almost wriggled free but Ike Claver, desperate to be free of his captivity, hurried to Lacey's assistance, bawling.

'Damn it, Jed, don't let that bastard slip the noose or we're dead men!'

Archer pounded his elbow into his tormentor's belly, and the rawhide necklace slackened some more. His hope of slipping the noose was short-lived. Ike Claver reached through the bars, grabbed a fistful of Archer's hair and hammered his head against the bars with as much force as he could. Then, with the marshal reeling, he took over from his partner and, showing no pity, tightened the noose around Archer's neck, relishing the man's demise.

Ben Archer felt the last vestige of strength ebb from him as stars exploded in front of his eyes and darkness took him.

'Gotcha, you old bastard!' Ike Claver neighed.

* * *

Jack Bannister's head was full of Kate Bonner's scent. His heart leaped and staggered and leaped again on seeing her milky nakedness. She stretched out on the bed, like a purring cat, laughing whorishly.

'If we're opening presents, Jack, how about it?'

* * *

Jed Lacey's breath rasped in his throat. He drew deep breaths to restore his spinning senses. Waspishly, he kicked out at Ben Archer's still form, his boot meeting him full in the face.

'No sense in kickin' a dead man,' Claver grumbled, dragging his partner in murder along with him to the door. On the way they collected a Greener, a pair of rifles and their six-guns. Ike Claver gingerly opened the law office door, his squinting eyes taking in the street an inch at the time.

'All clear,' he announced.

'Wait,' Lacey said. He returned to the cells, followed by a curious and anxious Claver, who kept asking,

'What're you doin', Jed?'

Lacey took the spanking new lariat off the hook on the door leading to the cells and unfurled it.

Again, Claver asked anxiously, 'What're you doin'?'

Jed Lacey explained. 'That bastard marshal got this brand-new rope to string me up with. And now, it's him who's goin' to be danglin' on it.'

'Well, do what you've got to do, and let's get outa here,' Ike Claver urged.

Stepping out on to the boardwalk, with Lacey hugging his coat-tails, the duo quickly sought the deeper cover of what had been the town's hardware-store, its front window now displaying a scattering of rusted pickaxes and shovels shrouded in cobwebs; there was no call any more for such goods.

'We've got to get us a coupla strong-winded nags,' Claver said, and door-dodged along Main to the livery.

Catching him up, Lacey said, 'I ain't goin' nowhere, Ike. It's goin' to be ball-freezin' in the mountains, and — '

'And what?' Claver groused. 'Better'n havin' 'em swing in the breeze, ain't it?'

'I gotta plan, Ike.' The killer smiled slyly.

'A plan? What kinda plan, Jed?'

'To take over this town, everything and everyone in it. Pick it cleaner than a carcass after a vultures' feast, then come spring move on.' Ike Claver's goggle-eyed reaction to his scheme angered Lacey. 'It ain't so fanciful as you think!'

'Ain't you forgettin' Archer's deputy?' Claver snorted. 'I seen his gunplay, Jed. And I sure don't wanna be 'round if he had cause to act up agin.'

'We kill him first,' Lacey said simply.

Claver shook his head as if he was in the company of a loco man.

'I'd rather crawl under a rock and kiss a rattler. You throw your life 'way if you want. But I'm hittin' the trail on the fastest hoofs I can find.' He stalked off into the icy wind, but after a few paces pulled up short. 'Where d'ya figure this deputy might be, Jed?'

Jed Lacey's eyes drifted to Kate Bonner's mellowly lit bedroom window.

Claver sighed. 'Lucky bastard!'

'When Bannister's worm bait,' Claver's partner in mayhem sneered, 'we'll get lucky, too, Ike.'

Ike Claver's tongue licked sore-caked lips, and his eyes glowed with the evil of his thoughts.

'Ya know, Jed. Mebbe stayin' 'round this burg ain't such a bad idea after all.'

Lacey's sneer deepened.

'Ya know, I think I'm goin' to enjoy Bannister's second woman even more'n I did his first!'

19

Gunhawk lay perfectly still, his breathing becoming calmer. Alongside him Kate, too, was getting her wind back. No words were needed, the silence did the talking. After a while, Kate slept, and Bannister got up and dressed. He tiptoed to the door, then paused to look back. The glow from the wood-burning stove bathed her silken body, teasing the voyeur with its shadow and light fickleness. He had done many hard things in his life, but leaving Kate Bonner was the most difficult of all. As the door clicked shut, Kate's sad, sea green eyes opened.

'Goodbye, Jack Bannister,' she whispered. 'God go with you.'

Downstairs, Bannister fortified himself against the numbing cold with a half-bottle of whiskey. He also hoped that the liquor would go some way to dulling the pain of leaving Kate Bonner. He ordered three more bottles of rot-gut to add to the half-bottle he'd got left, to ward off the freezing cold on the mountain trails.

'You ain't headed out, are yuh, Mr Bannister?' the bemused barkeep asked. 'A man would have to be loco to move on before the first melting at least. Ain't you waiting for Jed Lacey's hanging?'

'Don't like hangings.'

On his way out of the saloon, he paused to look back at the balcony where he'd first set eyes on Kate Bonner, in what now seemed an age ago, half hoping she might be there, and half hoping she would not be.

She wasn't.

He went out into the late evening gloom and headed straight for the livery, rejecting the notion of paying his respects to Ben Archer. He'd said his goodbyes and there was nothing else to say. He hoped that his horse, rested and fed on prime oats, would have the stamina to see him to the plains, and then on to the goodly sized town to the south, where he planned to chuck his gun and begin his new life. He had no hankering to go back to being a storekeeper; he now had trail-fever in his blood. Maybe cow-punching would be an option. Living with cows would be a welcome change to the scum he'd been living with over the years of revenge.

Maybe some day, too, he'd ride back up the mountain, when he was a more useful man than he was now. The kind of home-loving man that Kate Bonner deserved. She might not be around but, if that day came, he'd go searching for her.

* * *

Across the street from the Wagon Wheel, Jed Lacey and Ike Claver sank back into the shadows, watching Bannister's progress to the livery. Incredulously, Lacey observed, 'Looks like he's ridin' out.'

'Good riddance, I say,' Claver snorted. 'The town is now ours, Jed.'

Lacey's mood darkened. 'I want him dead, Ike. I don't wanna spend my days lookin' over my shoulder.'

'Why bring trouble on our heads?' Claver reasoned. 'Bannister will figure that, as planned, Archer will have strung ya up. He won't come lookin'.'

Claver's reasoning lightened his partner's mood.

'Yeah. He will, won't he?' Bad tempered, he kicked out at a stone. 'I'd still like to kill the bastard, though.'

The stone skittered right across Main and clattered under the boardwalk on the other side, only feet from Bannister.

'What'd'ya do a fool thing like that fer?' Ike Claver admonished, dragging Lacey deeper into the shadows as Bannister paused mid-stride and turned to look along the deserted street.

'He'll think it's the wind playing tricks,' Lacey opined hopefully. Then, trying to grab the Greener from Claver, said, 'Mebbe I should blast him right now, Ike.'

The outlaw held on firmly to the shotgun. 'You've a real bent for invitin' trouble on yerself, ain't ya?'

Jack Bannister strolled into the centre of the street, the wind flapping at his long coat. He stood and watched, a dark, sinister image. The wind, ever blowing to some degree, was sweeping debris before it, in a town that was oversupplied with detritus as deserted buildings came apart.

'Looks like somethin' from Hell, standin' there!' Ike Claver observed shakily. He brought the Greener level with Bannister.

'Blast him, Ike!' Lacey urged.

The outlaw was giving Lacey's suggestion active consideration when, on bending down, Gunhawk picked up a wedge of rotten wood that the wind had blown against his right boot. He tossed it in his hand for a moment, before throwing it away. This damn town is vanishing in the wind, he said to himself. Then he turned and continued on casually towards the livery.

The lurkers let their breath out slowly. Jed Lacey, weak at the knees, used the wall of the building behind him for support. They watched Bannister ride out, head down into the buffeting wind, hat pulled low over his eyes. Lacey hugged Ike Claver wildly.

'This town is ours now, Ike!' He stepped forward out of the shadows to look boldly up at Kate Bonner's window. 'And I know what I'm goin' to get me first!' Seeing his partner's worried frown, he asked, 'What're you lookin' so glum 'bout?'

Looking along Main, Claver said. 'Don't rightly know. But I gotta ghost's finger on my spine, Jed.'

★   ★   ★

Once outside town, Jack Bannister left the trail and headed up through a tumble of boulders to a redundant mine he'd seen on his way into town.

He rode into the mine and dismounted. 'Sorry. This is the best I can do right now,' he told the mare, and hitched the horse to a tree-root poking through the wall of the mine shaft. He took his rifle from its saddle scabbard, and hurried back outside to gather up broken tree branches to fill the opening to the mine to keep the worst of the bone-chilling wind out of the shaft. Chore completed, he quickly made his way back to the trail and made tracks for town. There had to be a reason for the marshal's office to be unlit. Archer had prisoners to watch over. 'And a man doesn't sit in the dark with vipers,' he murmured.

Reaching the edge of town, he slowed his pace and merged into the twilight to wait and listen, before making his way along to the law office. He paused outside the door with his ear to it and, hearing only silence, he eased the door open to peer into the dark interior. Not knowing what to expect, he closed the door as gently as he had opened it, and for a cautious moment waited in the dark.

'Ben?' he summoned in a hushed tone.

★ ★ ★

The sparse scattering of patrons in the saloon glanced up with lazy indifference at the two men who'd come in, but they were full of attention a second later when they saw who their visitors were. Ike Claver ruled the room with the Greener.

'This town and ev'rything in it is now ours, gents,' he announced. He let his snake-eyes glide over the shocked gathering. 'Any objecters?'

One old-timer, showing more courage than his compatriots, challenged hotly.

'Did you fellas kill Ben Archer?' His feistiness earned him a side-swipe from Claver that sent him spinning across the saloon, and one or two more of a similar mind quickly sat down.

Jed Lacey cackled. 'Oh, the marshal's hangin' 'round.'

'Whiskey, barkeep,' Claver ordered. 'And plenty of it!'

Lacey's gaze settled on the balcony overlooking the bar. 'I've got a diff'rent kinda thirst, Ike.'

Claver sniggered. 'Yeah. Don't be too long. I gotta hankerin' m'self.'

* * *

Bannister did not want to draw attention to the marshal's office by lighting a lamp; there was nothing as eye-catching as a light flaring in the dark. He poked his way through the inky gloom towards the cells. Once inside the cells and out of view from the street, he struck a match and leaped back from the bloated face and popping eyes that loomed up in its flickering light. The initial shock over, he stood stock-still looking at Ben Archer dangling on a rope, strung over the top of Jed Lacey's cell door, the man who was known to him as Luke Birch. A murderous fury took Bannister over.

'You should have given Birch a gun when I asked you to, Ben!' His mounting rage twisted his features. 'Look what being a Good Samaritan's got you!'

20

Anger spent, pity welled up in Jack Bannister for the man he'd only known a short few days but whom he considered a friend. He cut him loose and dropped him gently to the floor.

'Now I'm going to have to hunt him down, Ben.' His anger returned briefly. 'I wouldn't have to, if you'd stepped aside, stubborn old fool that you were.'

He placed Archer on a couch in the office before stepping cautiously back outside. His grey eyes, bleak as the landscape, searched the darkness for sign of the murderous duo he was now determined to dispatch. He was certain that Lacey and Claver were still in town. Ike Claver's horse was still in the livery. Maybe Claver had been clever enough to steal a horse, figuring that Bannister or whoever would discover the jail breakout would reckon on

Claver still being around, if his horse was, and waste time fruitlessly searching, while he and Lacey made tracks.

But Gunhawk did not think that either of the pair was that smart.

The snow, too, he'd noted on his way out of town, bore no new tracks, though snow-tracks quickly vanished. Of course they could have gone the other way, but that was unlikely, as that trail went higher into the mountains; it was not a trail that any sensible man would take with the weather getting more spiteful by the minute. Of course Ike Claver and Jed Lacey were not ordinary men; they spent their days dodging the law, riding tough, out-of-the-way trails that often led through country that other men would balk at, like the winter-shrouded mountains they now found themselves in. They'd know of places to hide out that law-abiding folk would never know existed, or if they found them by mistake, would not live to tell of their discovery.

'Yeah,' Bannister murmured grimly. 'The rats are still in town, I reckon.'

★ ★ ★

Kate Bonner's heart fluttered wildly as her bedroom door stealthily edged open. Had Jack Bannister changed his mind? Maybe not for her. It could be that the deteriorating weather had changed his mind for him, and Hope Wells was the better option until the weather grew kinder and milder. She didn't care what his reason for returning was. It would be a long winter, and she had enough confidence in her womanly ways to — come spring — have Jack Bannister thinking homely thoughts. She paused in dressing; Bannister had already seen her nakedness. Besides, she smiled, there was no time like the present to start persuading him that by leaving without her when the thaw came, he'd be throwing away a whole lot of pleasurable nights.

Kate skittishly yanked open the

bedroom door and froze. Jed Lacey shook like a tree in a storm, so potent was the impact of seeing Kate Bonner's naked breasts. Kate shook too, but for very different reasons.

'Well, now, hi-dee-do, Kate.'

She slapped away his hand as it reached for her right breast, recoiling in revulsion. He snarled:

'Kinda uppity, ain't ya, for a cathouse slut?' Kate backed into the room, paced by Lacey. 'Oh, I know you never *entertained*, Kate, 'cept special clients like Jack Bannister. But, seein' that Ike Claver and me now run this shit-hole town, me and him are now special clients, too, Miss Bonner.'

'Get out!' Kate spiritedly flung a scent bottle at Lacey's head. The swiftness of her action caught him by surprise, and though he ducked, the crystal bounced off his forehead, ripping off a sizeable patch of skin, before shattering on the wall behind him. He wiped away the blood that ran copiously into the hollow of his right eye and spilled down his cheek. His anger pulsated across the room, and Kate knew that her hasty action would only make her suffering at his hands all the meaner.

'I'm goin' to teach you a lesson you ain't never goin' to forgit,' the killer snarled.

'I'm Jack Bannister's woman. He'll rip your heart out,' she threatened.

The killer's sneer deepened. 'Bannister's gone, Kate. And the way I figure, come the thaw his bones will be found in some gulch or ravine.'

'Don't count on it,' Kate flung back. 'Jack Bannister's done a whole lot of surviving in the last five years.'

As he closed on her, circling like a predatory animal in for the kill, Kate resorted to an age-old fall-back for a woman in peril. She screamed as loud as her lungs would allow her. Knowing that it was a scream into an empty wilderness that held no rescuer.

★ ★ ★

Kate Bonner's scream pierced Jack Bannister's heart with the ferocity of an arrow. His eyes shot to Kate's bedroom window and the terrible tableau being enacted on the lamp-lit blind as she struggled with her attacker. He cursed his slow-wittedness; a woman like Kate Bonner would have been an irresistible prize for Lacey and Claver to claim.

He knew he had the element of surprise going for him. Lacey and Claver must have watched him leave town. Because they dared not act if he was still around.

Bannister quickly crossed the street and began to climb on to the overhang over the saloon porch, directly beneath Kate's bedroom window. Purchase on the snow-coated support beams was difficult to find, and he knew that it would be even harder, once he reached the slanting roof of the overhang, to hold his grip. His shoulder, wounded by Spike Ring in the skirmish with the Claver outfit, though not severely so, began to act up, and became a problem added to problems. He knew the riskiness of his approach; if he lost his hold and slid off the overhang, the ensuing ruckus of his tumble would alert the murderous duo and likely end his attempt to rescue Kate, before he got enough wind back to recover.

On hearing Kate's second scream, he strove to resist the temptation to scramble wildly upwards, knowing that impatience on his part could lead to disaster of the worst kind for Kate Bonner.

21

Bannister's hands, frozen, and bloodied by nails and frosted splinters every bit as sharp, clawed at the overhang's roof, desperately seeking a grip, while his legs encircling the support beam ached with the effort of holding the purchase they'd gained, but were losing fast. He knew that he had only seconds in which to haul himself on to the overhang, or slide back down the support beam. There was also the chance that his weight might just prove too much for the decrepit structure, and it would collapse like matchwood under him.

He was beginning to regret not having risked a rescue through the saloon itself, but if he had opted for that, and Ike Claver had impeded him, it would have sent a warning to Lacey and, with nothing to lose, at worst he would kill Kate Bonner out of spite, or render him helpless by taking Kate hostage.

A board on the overhang on which Bannister had got a tentative hold *twanged* free of its rusted nails and flapped, making a din that, he reckoned, Lacey or Claver had to hear, if not both of them. Noisy as it was, it was his only purchase on the overhang, and if he let go of it, he might not get another grip. He hauled himself on to the overhang and scrambled on to the flapping board to still its clatter. Alarmed, he saw the tableau on the lamp-lit blind pause, and then saw a man's upraised hand swing in an arc. He watched Kate's figure lurch out of view on the end of the blow, before Jed Lacey (Luke Birch to Bannister) tore the blind from the window to squint into the night. He had to work hard to resist the urge to lunge at the window and crash through, but Lacey had taken the precaution of coming to the window holding a cocked gun. If Bannister engaged in any hasty action, all Lacey had to do was pull the trigger.

He lay perfectly still on the overhang, not daring to breathe or twitch a muscle, hoping that the heavy snow together with the darkness would make him invisible to Lacey's prying eyes. The fact that Lacey was looking out from a lit room into the dark helped.

The killer tried to open the window but its frame, luckily for Bannister, was frozen solid. When, after a moment's further consideration, Lacey turned away from the window, Gunhawk drew breath into aching lungs and geared himself for the final push. Knowing that disaster for Kate was now only seconds away, he dug his fingernails into the overhang, forcing his mind to ignore the pain of shredding fingers and skinned knees, to haul himself up under the window. He glanced inside to see Lacey on the floor, astride Kate, holding her down while trying to undo his trousers. He ended her fierce fight with a pile-driving fist that left her out cold and at his mercy, of which there would be none.

Bannister clawed his way upright, fighting both the gusting wind that could not make up its mind as to which direction it wanted to blow from, and the ice-caked saloon wall. Once upright, if he managed it, he knew that his lunge through the window would have to be instant, or he'd lose his footing and totter off the overhang. He was almost thrown off balance anyway, by the sudden burst of gunfire from the saloon.

Annoyed at having his attention diverted from the pleasure at hand, Jed Lacey leapt off Kate, yanked the bedroom door open and hollered.

'What the hell's goin' on down there, Ike?'

'Just a little shootin' practice,' came the drunken reply.

Lacey slammed the door shut and spun around, his jaw dropping to his knees as he saw Jack Bannister's figure looming at the window, before crashing through it to roll on the floor. As he corkscrewed upwards, the Peacemaker flashed orange flame. The two bullets from Gunhawk's spitting iron smashed Lacey back through the door. He was still struggling to hold his pants up and grab his gun when Bannister's third shot ripped his throat out.

Ike Claver's survival instincts took over his whiskey-soaked brain and he vaulted the bar to dive for cover. His bullets cut the chandelier's chain to send it crashing to the floor, plunging the Wagon Wheel into pitch darkness, as Bannister appeared on the balcony. The oil-lamps exploded on contact with the floor, and in an instant a ferocious fire took hold, the flames eating voraciously through the rotten floorboards. The patrons scattered, most of them taking advantage of the fire and darkness to escape. The gusting wind that blew through the open doors whipped the flames to new heights. Bannister glanced back anxiously along the hall to Kate's room, knowing that in a short while the saloon would be a roaring inferno. Bottles on the shelves behind the bar were already exploding, their liquor soaking the floor would only feed the ferocity of the blaze as soon as the trails of liquid streaking across the floor met with fire.

Gunhawk knew that he'd have to finish the business in hand pronto.

He edged down the stairs, which were already licked by the leaping flames. Both barrels of Claver's Greener exploded and the stairs shook under the impact, some of them collapsing and adding to the fire. Bannister grabbed a drape and hoisted himself up as the stairs crumbled under him. The ripping cloth held for long enough to give him time to swing out and drop to the saloon floor, just outside the circle of fire. Ike Claver flung the shotgun aside and began peppering the floor around Bannister with his six-gun as he rolled away from the flames licking his boots. He felt the sting of lead on his right shin. A second bullet nicked his left elbow, and he realized how lucky he'd been so far.

Ike Claver was a gun-handy gent.

Flames were beginning to eat their way up the stairs, and soon the entire building would be alight. Kate would be cut off. Soon escape through her bedroom window would not be possible either, as the front wall of the saloon was already being licked by the flames.

Made cocky by his success, Ike Claver leapt on to the bar, eyes ablaze in anticipation of the evil pleasure that he reckoned was about to be his. It was the mistake that Bannister had hoped for. Claver offered himself as a clear target. Gunhawk's Peacemaker cleared leather faster than a lightning-fork going to ground. It barked and lifted Claver clear off the bartop and slammed him against the wall behind the bar, blood trailing in a gory line as he slid to the floor.

Bannister hobbled back upstairs, hugging the wall and hoping that the flaming stairs would hold out long enough for him to make the balcony which, as yet, was intact, but not for much longer. Just as he gained the balcony, the stairs collapsed in a fiery ball, sending up showers of sparks that ignited everything they touched. Every inch of the saloon was now ablaze.

Jack Bannister limped along the hall to Kate Bonner's room and burst through the door. Kate was sitting up groggily, nursing her jaw where Lacey's fist had landed. Without further ado he swept her up in his arms and with her arms looped around his neck, he jumped through the last narrow gap in a wall of flame engulfing the front of the saloon. At that moment flames erupted through the floorboards in several different places.

Flying through the air, cocooning Kate against him to protect her from the voracious flames, Jack welcomed the coolness of Hope Wells's latest blizzard as he crashed through the fire-engulfed overhang, to land in the softness of the fresh snow. Winded, they lay in the snow watching the Wagon Wheel burn.

'Bannister,' Kate murmured. 'I owe you my life.'

'That's OK,' he chuckled. 'You'll have a lifetime to pay me back. And I'm going to be around every second to see that you do.' He drew her into his arms. 'I guess that's a proposal, Kate Bonner.' He sighed. 'Now, if we only had a preacher . . . '

Finale

'Do you, Jack Bannister, take Kate Cecily — '

'Cecily?' Bannister laughed.

'I had an English aunt,' Kate said huffily.

' . . . Bonner,' Larry Winston, the undertaker-cum-doctor-cum-herbalist-cum-preacher-cum-all-things continued, 'to be your lawful wedded wife?'

'Say 'I do', Jack,' Kate ordered.

'You're going to be a real bossy kind of woman, you know that, Kate Bonner,' Bannister opined. 'And I do,' he told Winston.

The winter was long, but pleasurable. The spring was mild and pleasurable, too. On their way out of town the Bannisters stopped to say goodbye to an old friend. On leaving the cemetery, Bannister asked his wife:

'Do you know anything about growing oranges, Kate?'

'No,' she answered. 'But I'm sure we'll soon learn.'

Bannister craned his neck to look back as the wheels of a second wagon joined theirs. It was going to be a long trip to California with Larry Winston along. As they rolled out of Hope Wells, Kate said:

'I sure hope Larry's doctoring skills take in baby delivering, Jack.'

Jack Bannister's ear-splitting *yee-haaa*! would have had Ben Archer's unqualified approval.

We do hope that you have enjoyed reading this large print book.

Did you know that all of our titles are available for purchase?

We publish a wide range of high quality large print books including:
Romances, Mysteries, Classics
General Fiction
Non Fiction and Westerns

Special interest titles available in large print are:
The Little Oxford Dictionary
Music Book, Song Book
Hymn Book, Service Book

Also available from us courtesy of Oxford University Press:
Young Readers' Dictionary
(large print edition)
Young Readers' Thesaurus
(large print edition)

For further information or a free brochure, please contact us at:
Ulverscroft Large Print Books Ltd.,
The Green, Bradgate Road, Anstey,
Leicester, LE7 7FU, England.
Tel: (00 44) **0116 236 4325**
Fax: (00 44) **0116 234 0205**

Other titles in the
Linford Western Library:

THE CHISELLER

Tex Larrigan

Soon the paddle-steamer would be on its long journey down the Missouri River to St Louis. Now, all Saul Rhymer had to do was to play the last master-stroke of the evening. He looked at the mounting pile of gold and dollar bills and again at the cards in his hand. Then, looking around the table, he produced the deed to the goldmine in Montana. 'Let's play poker!' But little did he know how that journey back to St Louis would change his life so drastically.

THE ARIZONA KID

Andrew McBride

When former hired gun Calvin Taylor took the job of sheriff of Oxford County, New Mexico, it was for one reason only — to catch, or kill, the notorious Arizona Kid, and pick up the fifteen hundred dollars reward the governor had secretly offered. Taylor found himself on the trail of the infamous gang known as the Regulators, hunting down a man who'd once been his friend. The pursuit became, in every sense, a journey of death.

BULLETS IN BUZZARDS CREEK

Bret Rey

The discovery of a dead saloon girl is only the beginning of Sheriff Jeff Gilpin's problems. Fortunately, his old friend 'Doc' Holliday arrives in Buzzards Creek just as Gilpin is faced by an outlaw gang. In a dramatic shoot-out the sheriff kills their leader and Holliday's reputation scares the hell out of the others. But it isn't long before the outlaws return, when they know Holliday is not around, and Gilpin is alone against six men . . .

THE YANKEE HANGMAN

Cole Rickard

Dan Tate was given a virtually impossible task: to save the murderer Jack Williams from the condemned cell. Williams, scum that he was, held a secret that was dear to the Confederate cause. But if saving Williams would test all Dan's ingenuity, then his further mission called for immense courage and daring. His life was truly on the line and if he didn't succeed, Horace Honeywell, the Yankee Hangman would have the last word!

MISSOURI PALACE

S. J. Rodgers

When ex-lawman Jim Williams accepts the post of security officer on the *Missouri Palace* river-boat, he finds himself embroiled in a power struggle between Captain J. D. Harris and Jake Farrell, the murderous boss of Willow Flats, who will stop at nothing to add the giant sidepaddler to his fleet. Williams knows that with no one to back him up in a straight fight with Farrell's hired killers, he must hit them first and hit them hard to get out alive.

THE CONRAD POSSE

Frank Scarman

The Conrad Posse, the famous group that had set about cleaning up a territory infested by human predators, was disbanding. The names of the infamous pistolmen hunted down by the Posse were now mostly a roll-call of the dead, but the name of the much sought Frank Jago was not among them. That proved to be a fatal mistake for it was not long before Jago took to his old trail of robbery and murder. Violence bred violence, and soon death stalked the land.